Pope!

Pope!

First paperback edition printed 2016 in the United Kingdom
A catalogue record for this book is available from the British Library.

ISBN 978-0-9575090-8-5

Published by Bongo Duck Publishing

To my Italian friends who showed me
the real Italy and to my children
who I hope will one day seek out
their own home from home.

A t vói bän Italia.

A t aringrâzi.

PROLOGUE – MILANO

The lights snapped on abruptly, heralding yet another nauseating day in the world of the prisoner. Rising wearily from his uncomfortable plastic bed, he blinked groggily at the clock with painted arms that always showed the same time. Behind the useless timepiece, stiff curtains were permanently held open around a window frame. Looking out of the window they framed he could see it was another bright and windless day – not that it would be anything else of course - the conditions were always benign here. In truth, some days were hotter than others but that was the only real variable.

The prisoner left his abode as this was his wish and his one freedom for he was free to move outside his quarters during the early and late parts of day, (before and after the hoards of visitors descended).

This morning he embarked on a long walk, down the garden path to join the pavement that hugged the main road. In the time it took him to traverse that small distance, the world around him had suddenly awoken. Cars whizzed past at fantastic speeds, screaming along their chosen paths accompanied by a shrill high-pitched whine and an acrid smell of carbon and heated metal that filled the still air. In the distance trains thundered past like horizontal rockets before burrowing into the side of hills and mountains, their subterranean passage belied by a deep rumbling beneath his feet.

The prisoner took this exact walk every morning to stretch his legs and exercise his brain. The aching sameness of his surroundings allowed him to concentrate on finding a solution to his most immediate and pressing problem – how to escape from his incarceration.

Every morning on his preamble he always met exactly the same people, in exactly the same places but he knew this was not by chance. First would be the businessman, one foot far in front of the other, engaged in a hurried jog as he clutched his briefcase. Clearly he was late for work, he always was and always would be. Next he would pass the mother crouching down by the glassy pond with her two small children. Three sets of arms outstretched, as if hoping that this day the ducks would at last come forward to take the offering of grain from their rigid outstretched hands. Finally the prisoner would climb one of the steep hills that bordered his confines, his breathing rate increasing slightly as he trudged up the spongy slopes of immaculately manicured grass. At the summit he would rest, leaning against the shepherd as the shepherd himself leaned against his crook, staring out over the fields, looking after his lazy sleep. The prisoner himself stared intently back down the hill at the now distant businessman and beyond.

Suitably rested, a subtle smile crept across the face of the prisoner as he slowly made his way back to his enforced residence, passing what remained of the businessman who was now a neatly dismembered figure on the pavement.

On his return, as he closed the door behind him, he could see the first visitors emerging through the great opening that lay over the horizon. Their great shapes moved almost imperceptibly, as to him they moved at a much reduced speed.

Yet another 'Groundhog Day' awaited but at least his walk this morning had finally given him an idea that would surely result in his escape. He would put the plan in action tomorrow, once he had worked out the finer details.

Today he had learnt something. His powers had meant to be useless and impotent in this place but with much focus and determination he had learned that he still had a vestige of his once feared strength. It was a mere iota of what he had possessed but he hoped it would yet prove enough to secure his liberty. Until tomorrow then, a date that now could not come fast enough.

2

I

I-I – VATICANO

Vincenzo Basso was old and tired and he had grown weary of his work. In fact he was almost bored at times, not that he could admit that to anyone, for this job was like no other.

It was the best job in the world and yet often the worst and now he yearned for a release from his hectic schedule. He knew he could quit as his predecessor had done so before him but Vincenzo insisted death would be the only way he would leave his post and he was aware this was unlikely to occur naturally any time soon. He was relatively fit for his age. Doctors told him he could expect to live for another decade, perhaps even two. However this sprightly octogenarian suspected his tenure (and therefore his life) may be ended prematurely. He could not put his finger on why he knew this but it was a strong gut feeling that he could not shift. People who whispered in adjacent rooms, stopping as he walked in. Papers that were shuffled out of the way before he could see them and people he knew well acting out of character. These were all signs of something suspicious but nothing consequential. Merely the evidence of elderly paranoia or the onset of dementia people would say but Vincenzo knew in his heart it was so much more, it was part of a conspiracy that involved a mortal plot against his very being.

If he was right then he would indeed be given the early freedom he now desired, even though it would result in his murder. Unfortunately it would also result in the catholic world, maybe even the entire western world, being thrown into chaos. But then again he thought, maybe the church needed such a jolt.

He had thought about telling someone but if somebody was out to kill him, nobody would believe him anyway. Besides, they would argue that he had his own private army to protect him and a pharynx of state of the art surveillance equipment everywhere he went. Of course this was all very true and made the prospect his downfall by nefarious hands to be almost an impossibility...unless of course that danger came from within.

He could not predict what exactly what might happen after he was disposed of. All he knew for sure was that the only way he could exercise any control was to try to put certain things in action before his own death. He wanted to smile at the cunning of his plan and the reaction it would receive if it worked but the gravity of the situation forced him to keep a straight face. Anyway, he knew there was a chance it would not work and he would not live to see the outcome.

Vincenzo rose from his lavish chair. He had been sitting for only a few moments but he often felt uneasy when he was too comfortable for too long, thinking that someone in his position should not be afforded such luxuries.

Today was a rare rest day, a brief respite in his ever-hectic itinerary that he had little say in organising. Two days ago he had returned by private plane from Guatemala and was due to fly out the next day to the holy site at Santiago de Compestela in Northern Spain. At least this next trip was mercifully shorter than the half a day it took to come back from Central America. He placed a hand lightly on his stomach, feeling slightly queasy at the thought of the turbulence he often experienced on these airborne voyages. Despite the hundreds of air journeys he had now undertaken, his body had never become accustomed to the unsettling experience of flight. He had been raised in a poor part of Southern Italy near Naples and had never even seen a plane close up until very late in his life. Now he was forced to use them as others used taxis. The only solace was that during these trips he felt nearer to God, not that He could hear him any clearer, especially in these fearful days.

In an attempt to clear the subtle wave of nausea from the thought of another turbulent flight, Vincenzo made his way towards the great door that led to his personal outdoor space. The great door only emitted a small squeak as it swung inwards on its well-oiled hinges. He took a deep breath of the cooling dusk air as he stepped out into his private gardens. It had to be his favourite place in the world because here, in the heart of Rome, he could honestly believe he was out in the countryside of his native region of Campagnia. Tall Cyprus trees softened the harsh outlines of great buildings and partially occluded an overgrown rosebush that wound its way over the walls, mingling with vines planted centuries before at the edge of the large and ornate courtyard.

Sometimes Vincenzo would pause to smell the over-powering bouquet of the rose-petals or nibble on a tart grape but tonight he made a beeline for his favourite part of the gardens, a small maze constructed of tall manicured hedges that rose to just above the height of a man. Only here within the snaking angular pathways did he feel truly alone. There were many routes through the maze he could follow, some that led to the centre and others that were dead ends. He knew them all. He often wondered at the meaning of planting such a structure here, in one of the most religious places in the world. After all, it was the only maze he knew at a religious site. There were hundreds of labyrinths at churches across the world as they depicted just one path, the path to God, but this was an odd incongruity here, being a maze containing many paths. Slowly he walked, almost in meditation, outstretching his arms either side of him to feel the coarse and sometimes sharp prongs of the hedgerow as he worked his way through the familiar twists and turns, choosing to turn left or right when he reached a fork or a junction, his decisions purely being based on whim.

Suddenly the aged man dressed in white could feel he was not alone. For a fleeting moment he wondered if it was God by his side but he sensed that if He was with him, the more solid shape of a person was also present. Without fear Vincenzo turned around. It seemed his macabre suspicions had been not without foundation. He sank to his knees, head almost touching the ground as he prayed to God one last time. His killer was at least swift in his action, the old man feeling no pain as the razor sharp blade was swung almost silently down against the back of his neck and easily through the other side. Only the baked earth below stopped its progress with a dull thud. The murderer slunk away slowly, knowing there was no need for haste as he would not be caught. The frothing, oxygen-rich blood of his slain victim flowed quickly from his severed neck, coagulating with the dry earth as it spread out to fill the width of the narrow passageway. The parched hedgerows at either side were grateful of the nutritious liquid feed, uncaring of its deadly origins.

I-II – VENEZIA

Luca opened his eyes with apprehension, in the same way some people do when awaking from an operation, unsure if they have woken up too early. His view was of a dark room, its high ceiling well above the horizon formed by the foot of the bed in which he led. Initially everything was unfamiliar but gradually his brain began to make sense of the world around him, despite the feeling that his grey matter was drowning in the poisonous by-products of all the sickly sweet cocktails he had drunk the previous evening.

He tried not to remember the sordid events of the last few hours that now punctuated his thoughts with each painful pulse of his pounding headache, as it was an all too familiar tale. Before he dared to move there was a stirring beside him from under the embroidered silk blanket. Instinctively he recoiled slightly, fearing a loving or lustful touch (which was worse he thought?) from his carnal companion who still slumbered contentedly beside him. Clearly she was still revelling in the dream that for him was now more like a nightmare.

Slowly he slid himself out of the bed in one limber move that was designed to not awaken the other occupant of the mattress. Luckily the slippery silk aided his smooth passage and his female companion (of more mature years and slightly sallowing skin) was not roused. Luca silently gained some distance between their naked bodies and easily found his clothes. Regardless of his state when retiring to an unfamiliar bed, he always somehow retained the where-with-all to pile his clothes together near the door. His precautions always made for an easy get away in the small hours, avoiding an awkward goodbye in the morning. Scooping up his vestments he flinched at a movement in the corner of the boudoir. He relaxed when he realised it was merely his own reflection and not his awakening partner. He did not pause to look at his reflection but made a hasty exit.

The lady who had so enjoyed his company the previous evening only realised his covert departure a couple of hours later when she reached over to feel the other half of the bed, now empty and cooling. She mused that it could almost have been a very pleasant dream if it wasn't for the dent in her husband's wallet. Still, he would not notice the missing notes even though sometimes she wished he would and ask why.

With every silent step down the carpeted staircase, Luca erased another wisp of memory of the nocturnal events from his mind. Holding his shoes in one hand, he looked down at his feet as he trod carefully in his holey odd socks.

Suddenly he was reminded of being a young child. Then as now he found it difficult to sleep and often snuck down the stairs at night in his stockinged feet when his patents were asleep. He would creep towards the window and carefully open the rusting shutters, trying to not make a sound that would rouse anyone. Seated on his favourite cushion he would spend hours watching the river traffic, often being awoken in the morning by a clip around the ear from his father who found him curled up and fast asleep by the open window.

At night Venice sleeps and so does its lifeblood, its network of canals. There are no noisy chugging river buses (*vaporetti*) ferrying locals and the more numerous tourists around the various sights. The slender and silent gondolas are safely moored against their poles adorned with coloured stripes and private speed boats and expensive river taxis no longer speed past. The young Luca was therefore starved of the boats he loved by watching the canal at night. He had to make do with sparse offerings of infrequent goods craft that delivered expensive produce and other fineries for the demanding patrons of the numerous exclusive hotels. Occasionally though a fire boat or ambulance would briefly break the silence and illuminate the surrounding buildings with pulses of red or blue before quickly disappearing from his field of view around the curve in the canal. Of course he would have preferred the chaos and wondrous colour and life that oozed from the daytime traffic on the canal, especially the handsome men on gondolas as they gracefully jostled for position with the motorized giants with whom they were forced to share the narrow waterways. Luca never had the time or the opportunity though as during the day he was forced to go to school or perform chores for his mother.

By the time he reached adulthood Luca had given up his night-time viewings for a new endeavour and although it put money in his pocket he knew it was something he should stop because of the way it always made him feel, the morning after the deed. The terrible hangover, a consequence of establishing the required Dutch courage, was bad enough but the accompanied gut-wrenching feeling of guilt and shame was many degrees more sickening.

Not many knew what he got up to behind the closed doors of Venice's more salubrious establishments after nightfall but those that did were largely supportive. It was simply a 'business transaction' they tried to say and that he was 'providing a service'. Maybe so but that was a cold way of looking at what was an emotional game that he played, tugging at the heart-strings of bored and sex-starved women of a certain age.

The women knew what they were doing and were always happy to hand over the money but, in almost every case, they looked for that suggestion of lust or even adoration in the eyes of him, their escort. That was the problem for Luca as for some reason, at some point, he had started playing up to that hope, hope that was always cruelly snuffed out like a candle thrown into the murky waters below when he left them during the night without a word, a kiss or a note.

Using the crumbling back doors Luca left the hotel utterly unnoticed. Breathing a sigh of relief at another well-executed escape he walked briskly along the narrow brick-lined passageway, pausing only to muse at the way canal front buildings were constructed. The cheap, drab workman-like brick was hidden here around the back, away from all the adorning eyes. For centuries visitors passed by and entered the great buildings by the far more grand marble clad facade at the front. Only tradesmen and servants ever saw the shabby rear where there was no need for such expensive fineries. In truth even the fronts were merely a façade as in reality the *whole* building was made of brick. Only a thin veneer of stone and marble at the front covered the truth. The reason for this was two-fold. Firstly, a slender marble skin was often all the owners could afford and secondly, buildings in Venice were rarely constructed wholly of stone as the weight would probably cause the whole construction to sink into the lagoon mud beneath its yielding and waterlogged foundations. The beauty of Venice was therefore skin deep. The great lady wore a fantastically painted mask but look around the back and the telltale signs of old age, like fine wrinkles and sagging skin, was always visible.

The first rays of morning light that greeted Luca were not of a hue that would cause Renaissance painters to slam down their Grappa or throw down their muse in order to scrabble for their paints and easels to capture the scene. The colour was a murky green-grey that blanketed the middle distance and beyond, washing the buildings in a monochrome livery that only enthusiasts of Turner would appreciate. The timid sun was somewhere just above the horizon but its position could not be determined through the bank of fog that the giant orb was clearly reluctant to penetrate. Making light of the eerie conditions, Luca strode confidently on, the click of his shoes on the flagstones rebounding back off the fog as if the suspended water droplets hid solid walls. He was not too familiar with the hotel where he had just spent the night but a Venetian is never lost for long in their own city and soon enough he reached a familiar street and knew he was nearly home.

A glance at his expensive watch (a gift from another grateful customer whose looks or name he had long since forgotten) showed he had a couple of hours before he had to get ready for work. This would just afford him a little shut-eye before the fairground that was Venice cranked into life again. One final bridge to traverse and then home. The city was still just asleep as he crossed a typical metal footbridge, one that could be found in all the iconic photos of Venice. (Ironic he thought, as they were thought of as new and vulgar when they were installed a century or more before). As he reached his front door he was watched by a group of tame sparrows, the small birds taking a break from scouring the floor for any breadcrumbs left from the day before. In the canal just further on, a tired and battered lemon bobbed by on the tide. The water around the sullen fruit glooped and gurgled as it met the steps that led down to the water's edge and continued under its surface, built to reach a water level that was once much lower.

Luca fell into a grateful sleep almost as soon as his head hit the pillow. Meanwhile, the tired lemon that had spent many hours wending its way east with the purging outward tide, had almost reached the open lagoon when a rising swell signalled the changing of the tides. Without a struggle it had no choice but to join the fresh waters from the Adriatic as they began to infiltrate the city once more. With the new life blood of fresh salt water gently flooding through the arteries of the old naval stronghold, it's inhabitants, (tourists outnumbering locals by four to one or more), awoke for another day at the greatest show on earth.

An unwelcome alarm assaulted Luca's ears. It was a bell he was sadly very used to but it still took him a while to recognise the ugly sound and even longer to elucidate its significance. Slowly Luca slid his corpse out of bed, never rising far from the mattress and stooping as he padded the short distance to the bathroom as if he was as old as he felt at that moment. By the time he was washed and dressed he at least felt a modicum of life crawl back into his vital systems as he headed for his front door, almost forgetting to lock it as he started on the familiar short route to work. It was another day he was sure would be just like any other, just like Disneyland he often thought. The weather may change constantly and all four seasons could easily be experienced in one day, but the numerous wide-eyed tourists were always the same. At least for him that resulted in a constant and reliable stream of potential customers. Luca only took two steps before being accosted. Luckily it was only the postman who demanded his signature for a letter sent by recorded delivery. Too hung-over to even be the slightest bit intrigued by this unexpected delivery and too late for work to throw it back in his house for later perusal, he stuffed the envelope in his jacket pocket to scan later at a more convenient time.

It was still early and the 117 islands that make up Venice were bereft of tourists who would later smother every central thoroughfare, rushing past centuries of history but not seeing the true Venice of today. They would choose to avoid the drab houses of the back streets with the poor children playing outside underneath bulging washing lines strung between the tenements. They would be oblivious to the crowded movable metal boards used for political posters declaring the latest would-be local champion to take on the powers of far away Rome and uncaring of the small wooden carts overflowing with vegetables grown by female inmates at the nearby prison island, the seller harangued by a phalanx of indomitable matriarchs determined to secure a bargain.

However, there was still plenty of activity at this hour, especially in the heart of Venice at the ancient Rialto market. The fish traders, the early risers of market tradesmen, were busy setting up their stalls of fresh fish and seafood for the locals and the restaurants. A couple of the older sea dogs looked away as he passed. As a gondolier he was looked down upon by the older generation as a panderer to the tourists and not a man with a real trade. Weaving past the last of the fisherman, he was forced to jump clear of the speeding contents of a bloodstained box of melting ice before he reached his destination. It was unclear whether the stall owner had intended to soak his brogues but Luca did not fancy an argument that morning and walked on instead of looking back with a confrontational glare. Luca slowed as he reached the tiny square that was hemmed in by a church with a large one-armed clock face on one side and commercial buildings on the other three. Behind one corner of the church the Rialto bridge rose obliquely, two-thirds of its span obscured from view. To his right, a market was strung along the walkway at the edge of the square, lying in wait for the hoards that would later march off the bridge in their thousands. Opting to remain in the square, Luca dragged a battered stool up to a small booth and heavily sat down next to another male youth already seated. The other man faced away from Luca but he did not need to see his front to know the back was owned by his colleague of many years. He had known him long enough to be a friend but a colleague he remained, as friends are people you like, not those you despise.

The colleague, Sergio Amalfi, did not turn to look at Luca but raised his head and sniffed the air like a dog suddenly picking up the scent of cooking sausages.

"What a beautiful morning we have today Luca, I can smell money in the very air today".

Luca did not respond but merely raised two fingers to the man inside the booth who nodded economically and slapped down two glasses of colourless grappa in front of them.

"Money that you always threaten to let slip between your fingers my dear Luca, as every day we meet here and every day you are late. Think of the wealth we could be accruing right now!" continued Sergio.

Luca downed his grappa in one swift swig, his face contracting as the harsh liquid scorched his throat. "There are no tourists up at this hour, you know that Sergio."

"Maybe true my friend but if we do not make haste we will not be there at the canal side when the first tourists do arrive and our wily competitors will take advantage of our absence. You need to be more business-minded my dear Luca, like the modern Venice. Take this church in front of us as a prime example." Sergio gestured lazily towards the façade of the church. "I doubt you know but this is probably the oldest church in Venice, still standing after fifteen hundred years." Sergio paused to allow Luca to be impressed but he merely shrugged. Sergio continued unabashed.

"One hundred years ago, this church was on its knees. Falling attendances, falling revenue and falling masonry and so without the money for repairs it started falling down. Even the famous one-armed twenty-four clock stopped revolving. So, what did the church do in the first instance?"

Luca's thumping head hoped this was a rhetorical question. Whether it was or not, Sergio saved him the effort of replying.

"The church cut costs and just opened it once a year for services. Completely the wrong decision but then they were still treating it as a church!"

"But it is a church," interjected Luca.

Sergio looked back with scorn as if a heckler had just interrupted a presidential address. "No, not any more Luca. At least that is not now its primary function. You see, the great Catholic Church realized its failings and sold itself to the Gods of commerce. This church and thousands others around the world is now open every day, not as a functioning church but as a museum! The mighty Catholic church has realized the assets it has is the key to maintaining power and wealth in these times, using its buildings to raise money through gawping tourists who pay homage to architecture rather than the almighty. Anyway, that is my business lesson over for today. Come, let us seize the day!"

Standing up suddenly, Sergio toppled his stool behind him, picked up his glass and downed his drink in one glug. Luca, who had already sunk his tipple, arose less dramatically before they strode off together towards the canal bank where their gondolas were moored.

Luca hated working with Sergio but, financially, he knew he had little choice as they simply worked so well as a team. Or, more exactly, they had an arrangement that suited both parties. In many ways the two young men were polar opposites. Sergio was a granite-jawed Adonis of a man with jet-black hair offset by striking blue eyes. Luca was not ugly but a female equivalent may have been politely called 'plain'. By his own admission Luca had an ordinary face with eyes slightly too close together, centred by an unsightly large and crooked nose, a combination of facial features not generally considered to be classically attractive.

Luca benefited in the relationship as Sergio was the willing ringmaster of the operation. As the confident one, he would happily call out to the passers-by, tempting them in with his deep baritone voice and promises of 'special offers' and 'discounts' which were not actually anything of the sort. The types of gondolas they rode could only hold two or three people at most, so families were often split up for their rides between the two colleagues, giving Luca trade that he probably would not have obtained on his own with his quiet demeanour.

Sergio also profited in their joint venture. Many days he would be in a bad mood or too impatient. On other days his confidence would come across to potential punters as brashness or over-eagerness. Either way, potential customers would be lost as they frowned and hurried away in search of a less surly boatman. On these occasions Luca would step in as the more gentile of the two to calm the ways.

After each seesaw day, the proceeds of both boats were split between them equally. When one had a bad day, the other invariably had a good one so it resulted in more of a steady intake for both bachelor's silk-lined pockets.

As Luca had expected, despite Sergio's haste, they had to wait almost an hour for their first fare to appear. An hour he could have quite happily spent in bed.

Their first customers of the morning were at least typical and therefore undemanding. They arrived in the plump form of a middle-aged German woman and her two, far more shapely, adolescent daughters. The siblings were clearly delighted that their mother had chosen a pair of gondoliers that included Sergio as they were clearly immediately captivated by his looks and beaming smile. Luca was barely noticed at his side. In a well-rehearsed spiel, Sergio quickly convinced the mother that the two daughters would be safe with him whilst he also ensured her that Luca would take care of her individual needs. Luca sighed inwardly as he predicted (with some confidence based on past experiences) how the day would unfold from this point forward.

Sergio's biceps tensed unnecessarily as he thrust his oar into the lagoon mud to cast off, the two girls transfixed by every ripple of his steely arms. In Luca's boat, the mother waved excitedly at her daughters as he cast off himself, the embarrassment of his own weaker forearms covered by his longer sleeves.

Luca allowed Sergio to forge ahead, affording him just enough of a gap between the boats so that the predator could casually ask the girls which hotel they were staying at without the mother overhearing (and rightly) judging his intentions. At the same time, the mother turned back to Luca with a look that told him he would get much more than the name of her hotel if he asked. He returned a polite smile, not taking the bait. He decided he'd had enough of those types of liaisons for a while.

He pushed on towards Sergio's identical slender craft, jealousy the fuel that drove him to curtail his colleague's private moment with the young sisters, wishing he had the looks to get noticed by the women his age and not their divorced mothers. Luca's pursuit was slowed however as he became distracted by a colourful butterfly that fluttered down out of the sky before coming to rest on the prow of the boat. Seemingly unabashed it basked, absorbing energy from the black surface of the gondola that was already being heated by the morning sun that had begun to pierce the earlier fog. Luca mused at the fragile creature and remembered an analogy he had once been taught by an old sea captain he knew.

The story he was told was that of a butterfly that starts life as a humble dirt brown caterpillar. Quietly it crawls through its short life, trying to be ignored by the rest of the world before time would come for its transformation. The small creature would cocoon itself away in a protective environment whilst it underwent the change, only to emerge again. However, the being that now paraded itself was very different to what it was before as the whole world would now take notice of its new radiant form. The dull caterpillar was now a dazzling butterfly that would spread its symmetrical wings, their shape seemingly thrown together elegantly with a succession of gentle Mandelbrot curves and points. Iridescent patterns of bright colours would dazzle those who looked and some would even be mesmerised by a pair of false eye on the wings that threatened to swallow every voyeur whole like a dizzying whirlpool in a deep blue ocean. Those that dared to obtain such a fine specimen as this were, alas, almost always disappointed. Victims would be lured in by the gently flapping wings, the undulating movements of the brightly liveried appendages like a beckoning finger to the willing pursuer. The suitor would stealthily creep up close and reach out for their quarry only for the delicate creature to teasingly fly away at the last moment. Subsequent attempts at capture would always produce the same result. The butterfly would always land again some short distance away and rest briefly, teasing those that chased by displaying its wares again only to leap into the air with split-second timing to once again evade being ensnared. The lucky few that did manage to trap the beautiful beings would often damage their delicate structure as they did so, rubbing the very colour from their wings or subduing their nature irreversibly.

Luca was not a successful butterfly catcher and he knew he never would be. He would have to make do with dull and dusty moths that flew blindly into his light at night, helpless due to their age, delirium caused by intoxication or a sad misplaced romanticism.

Luca brought himself back to the 'real' world. Once again he felt the gently swaying wooden boat beneath his feet and the long oar in his hands. Daydreaming, he had been on autopilot, almost unconsciously steering through the quiet canals.

Looking down at the dusty fat 'moth' in his boat, it was clear she had long since given up flying towards his light. After quickly growing bored at failing to attract his attention she now wore a sullen expression, probably envious of her daughters, full of youth and the more attractive opportunities that brought. He followed the gaze of the middle-aged lady towards Sergio, his white teeth clearly visible as he smiled and joked with his two adolescent guests who were both blushing a shade of peach more commonly seen in a local Bellini cocktail. Luca made a slight snarl as he wondered what florid compliment Sergio had just made to elicit such a fawning response from the siblings. Not for the first time today Luca wished his colleague ill winds. Sergio was the alpha male, the Venetian lion who sailed easily through life whereas Luca was forever ploughing through choppy waters. There was no way Luca could be blamed for what happened next but those with superstitious beliefs would say he would almost immediately regret such malicious musings.

Glancing at his watch, Luca realised that half an hour had passed since they had set off. It was time to turn back. The three ladies had paid for an hour and these particular gondoliers were not in the habit of giving their time for free. Jamming his oar into the mud he pivoted and turned the slender craft around. Normally it was Sergio who led the return journey but today the alpha male was happy to take the back position, probably still trying to tease out from his young patrons the name of the hotel where they were staying that night. Luca smiled at the possibility of Sergio not getting what he wanted for once.

They had not punted more than a few lengths of the return leg before Luca noticed an empty stretch of canal branching off to his left, the narrower waterway cordoned off with the traditional wooden pillars embedded in clay. The other end of the short stretch of drained naval passageway could be spied in the near distance, a matching barrier keeping the water out. Although the space in between had been pumped away, the bed was far from dry but filled with the putrid black mud on which Venice was built.

Purging stretches of canal such as this was an everyday event in Venice. A constant rolling programme of works continued all year round to inspect the walls of the canals for leaks and to strengthen their sides against the ever-rising tides they were not designed to withstand. Something was different about these particular set of works though. They had obviously been commissioned in a great hurry as Luca did not remember the canal being dry the day before and there was none of the usual notices warning boats that maintenance was about to take place. Luca could only conclude that a basement in one of the adjoining buildings must have flooded overnight. (Many lower basements in the city were permanently flooded due to the combined effects of rising water levels and the sinking buildings but a leak in an upper basement was more serious as the water level could continue to rise into the living quarters if the offending hole was not plugged). He suspected that the owner of this particular palazzo must be particularly well off and had friends in high places to have the hole fixed so hastily. Typically there were no workers present at that moment, probably taking one of their frequent breaks for a fortifying shot of espresso or grappa.

Luca sailed on but looked back to ensure that his colleague was following and not absconding with the two maidens. This time he was indeed obediently behind him sporting a huge knowing grin at Luca as he dangled a hotel room key from his fingers. That cad had worked even quicker than he expected, thought Luca. He could not bear to look at Sergio any longer, not knowing what angered him more, the brazen success of the other man or the fact that Sergio revelled in the envy Luca felt.

Behind him Luca could hear the calm measured strokes of the gondolier's oar synchronised with his own smooth movements but it was a synchrony that did not last long. Suddenly the physical actions of his colleague were a desperate and irregular thrashing as Sergio attempted to propel the narrow craft as quickly as he could muster. Luca looked back. The smile had been wiped from Sergio's face, replaced by open-mouthed horror. The girls in the boat began to shriek as his frantic movements rocked the narrow gondola in an alarming manner. Luca could see Sergio was scared out of his skin. Luca froze, looking on with bewilderment. He could not see what the danger was but he only had to wait a moment longer to discover what had so spooked the other gondolier.

From somewhere behind the damned canal, a blinding flash of light briefly competed with the hazy sunshine. A bolus of smoke mushroomed from the same spot and then the world began to tilt as if the water around them was being sucked away and into the now open void. Luca was far enough away from the phenomenon for the effect on his boat to be minimal. As his watering eyes began to recover from the blinding blast, all he felt was the slight tug of a strong tide on his craft. Instinctively he rowed towards the canal bank and tied the boat securely to a nearby mooring. The rope strained against the pull of the withdrawing waters but it held firm.

Sergio was not so lucky. His boat began to tip backwards and was carried serenely towards a new waterfall as if it were a twig. Valiantly he continued to pound the waters with his oar but the force of the rushing torrent was more than a match for his strength. Luca could only watch on helplessly as all three on board disappeared through a jagged aperture of splintered wood and metal and on to the unseen swirling waters on the other side. Part of Luca wanted to dive in despite the dangers to rescue the stricken trio but a greater part made him freeze where he was with the now distraught mother, his sense of self-preservation taking precedence.

Even then he knew he would have to live for a lifetime with the subsequent guilt of the decision he had made in those fleeting moments. At least the ringing in his ears caused by the explosion spared him from hearing the final plaintive screams of the stricken threesome.

Soon the waters calmed as an equilibrium was reached between the two bodies of water either side of the wrecked works. Gripped by a renewed haste and powered by adrenalin, Luca quickly untied his boat and raced over to the scene of devastation. What he saw at first confused him and then sent an icy chill through his body. One of the girls was still in the water but resting her arms on the paved bank like an exhausted swimmer after a long race, the clothes on her back ripped to shreds and welts blossoming beneath. She was battered and bruised but appeared to be in no real danger. Her sister had fared even better and had hauled herself onto the bank. She was crouching down over a jumble of ragged clothes spread out in a line. As Luca advanced he could see that the jumble of garments was actually the motionless form of his work partner, Sergio, the other sister frantically attempting to revive him by performing mouth-to-mouth resuscitation.

Luca always thought that Venice was in the wrong place when it came to the setting of the sun. How picturesque would it be for those evening visitors arriving on the train or by car to be presented with the city bathed in a fiery orange glow that slowly sank into the Adriatic in the east. Instead it was the daily fleeing hoards that made do with the sun descending almost shamefully behind the industrial smoking chimneys that the coastal town of Mestre had to offer in the west. Ignoring that bleak sunset Luca skulked in his train seat as his thoughts inevitably returned to the day his life changed.

Sergio never made it past that day. Briefly he was brought back to the living by the kiss of life from the beautiful daughter and was rushed to hospital by ambulance boat but he stopped breathing again on route and despite more frantic efforts to revive him he was pronounced dead on arrival. Luca had obviously been questioned as a suspect by the police. It was well known he had not seen eye-to-eye with Sergio and he was at the crime scene as the events unfolded. However, after a fraught couple of days and nights of interrogation and sleeping in a dank cell, the inspector had to let him go due to lack of a real motive and evidence. The policeman was clearly reluctant as there were no other leads after forensics had drawn a blank at the bombsite and no useful witnesses had come forward.

As soon as he left the police station, Luca went home and packed what few possessions he considered valuable and was now on the first train out of Venice. He did not want anything more to do with that doomed city. It had been his home all his life but perhaps the unfortunate events of the other day was the catalyst he needed for change in his life. He knew it would look like he was running away with a guilty conscience but people could think and say what they liked behind his back as he knew he was not to blame. The alternative would have been less than palatable anyway. Venetians were a suspicious and superstitious people. He would surely have been harangued out of his job one way or another as no other gondolier would want to be within a canal width of him. Those that didn't think he was a slayer of gondoliers would blame the incident on bad luck or even a curse.

The police could not find a trace of explosives in the drained canal that day so could only conclude the explosion was caused by a gas leak, even though none of the locals had reported smelling anything out of the ordinary. Luca could not help by ponder another possibility though. If the explosion was malicious then had he been the real target and not Sergio? It was him and not his colleague that should have been the rear boat at that moment as he always normally followed Sergio back to their mooring posts. But if the deadly explosion really was meant for him, then why?

He crossed his arms and slumped further in his seat, fatigue from the lack of sleep and stress catching up with him as his eyelids became heavy. He was just nodding off as he heard a crinkling sound from the inside pocket of his jacket. Peering into the pouch he produced the letter he had been given that morning by the postman. Unsurprisingly he had completely forgotten about it. Opening the slightly water damaged envelope he slid out its only contents, a small printed card. Confusion changed to humour and disbelief as he read the invitation. It must be a hoax he thought, but what did he have to lose in finding out? It was time to leave Venice, possibly for good, and this invitation at least gave him a clear destination to head for.

I-III – VATICANO

The Cardinal Camerlengo (or Pope's chamberlain as he is more commonly known) sat behind his bare, unpolished wooden desk, poring over the accounts of His Holiness. Keeping the personal finances of the Pope solvent was one of his many menial tasks but it was one he enjoyed with relish as, because of the position of absolute trust that went with the role, he could easily transfer a few thousand Euros every month to his own personal account without fear of being discovered. What the Camerlengo had planned next though would make such thieving look like stealing a single coin thrown by a tourist into the Trevi fountains in search of good fortune.

As the trusted chamberlain saved the computer spreadsheet he was working on and started a game of Solitaire he heard determined footsteps echoing along the corridor to the left of the room where he sat. He craned his neck eagerly, curious as to the owner of the footsteps who was about to appear in the open doorway. His quickening heart belied the importance of who was about to glide into view and what they were about to say. At least the footfalls were slow, steady and measured. A running man would have almost certainly been the bearer of bad news and would have made the Camerlengo reach for the gun he had recently taped underneath his desk.

A Swiss Guard appeared in the doorway, still wringing his hands with a cloth stained with bright red patches. His calm demeanour made him look for all the world like a mechanic who had just completed a simple oil change on a two-stroke engine. Only the telltale hue of the stained rag showed that the worker had recently been covered in blood and not sump oil.

The Camerlengo sprang up from the desk, planting his sweaty hands palm down on its surface, the rough wood below meekly accepting the moisture into its old timbers. "Is it done?" he shouted nervously, covertness not required in these soundproofed and firmly locked chambers.

"It is done Camerlengo. *Il Papa è morto*". The Pope is dead.

I-IV – ROMA

Laura was standing dutifully in the pouring rain but she really didn't know why anymore. Her expensively curled hair now resembled rat's tails, her carefully applied make-up clearly wasn't as waterproof as it promised and her thin chiffon dress clung to her skin like a swimsuit after a dip in the sea on a cold day. To top it all, her new shoes (costing a month's wages) were being ruined by the foam bubbling up from the recently shampooed red carpet beneath her. She glanced at her watch, praying for the delicate gold hands to speed up before looking up and squeezing out a forced smile as an elderly but gentrified couple rushed past her into the dry and warm sanctuary of the cinema, politely declining the programme she proffered. (On instructions from her boss, each paper guide was protected from the elements in its on plastic wallet, a level of protection she had not cared to provide for her own assistant who cursed herself one more time for forgetting an umbrella.)

Laura waited until the door closed behind the geriatrics before wiping the smile from her face as if it had never been there. Yet another glance at the watch told her she had only ten more minutes of this soaking humiliation before she too could join them and the other chosen dignitaries inside to take her place at the very back of the theatre on a make-shift seat normally reserved for humble ushers.

It had promised to be one of the highlights of the summer season for anyone who was anyone in Rome. Famous faces from film, TV and local politicians had been expected to grace this little film premiere with their presence, accompanied by their wives or mistresses (depending on preference or occasion). The only issue was someone clearly forgot to invite the sun. As early evening arrived with a cool, relieving breeze from the west, it also brought with it dark and brooding storm clouds that erupted just as the invited guests were at home adjusting their neck ties and strapless dresses. The vast majority of the famously fickle Rome social scene looked out of their ornate windows and decided to stay in rather than brave the elements, leaving their caligraphied invite on their dressing tables as they opted for a night in.

Laura did not care that the cinema tonight would barely be one-fifth full. All she cared about at that time was being warm and dry and wishing she was back home at her flat, stroking her adoring cat and maybe smoking a spliff as she watched the clouds roll past until the fading light made them impossible to discern against the night sky.

At last she got the signal from her boss, ushering her inside with almost a scolding, as if she should have abandoned her posting on the red carpet hours ago. Laura found her allocated seat in the corner at the back of the theatre, well away from her boss and the other dignitaries. Her view was even obstructed by a pillar but her gradually warming and drying body was her only care now. Besides, it was a terrible film anyway.

Rainwater absorbed by her dress began to drip onto a few kernels of forgotten sticky popcorn strewn over the worn carpet at her feet as she absently glanced at her ticket in the dim light. Turning it over she saw something that surprised her on the reverse of the card. Someone had placed a large sticker on the back, printed with elaborate text. She was curious but she thought it was probably just an advert aimed at the guests. She slotted the invite into her handbag to read later as the lights dimmed to almost complete darkness. As the opening credits finally rolled, many of those who had brought a mistress began to enjoy their special time together whereas most of those who had brought their wives endured the next two hours in silence.

Laura had been delighted when she had landed this job almost a year and a half before. As an assistant to the head of the biggest film promotion company in Italy she thought this would be an excellent opportunity to secure a foothold on the first rung of the ladder in the film business, the start of her dream career.

Her desire to make it in the film industry was no surprise considering her childhood. As the father of a successful actor (albeit one who only starred in moderately successful historical television movies) she spent a lot of her time either watching him on television or, when longer shoots were involved, following him around the country on location. Her mother would help to school her on these unusual sojourns, in between performing her role as cook for the cast and crew. It was a fascinating life for a child who was constantly in awe of the colourful characters (on and off the screen) who were often dressed in flamboyant outfits performing stunts and daring action scenes.

It was a nomadic lifestyle that seemed normal to Laura until she was twelve years old when her father landed a major part in a popular soap opera set in the beautiful Tuscan city of Lucca, near Pisa. At first Laura struggled to come to terms with a permanent home but in time she settled at school, learning to make friends and before long she began to thrive in her formative years.

For all her life to this point Laura had lived in a fabricated environment of kings and queens, emperors, magicians and wizards and despite the dose of reality administered by now living in a fixed abode, the city of Lucca only added to her 'fantasy world' outlook on life. Entering the outskirts of the city, you could be forgiven for thinking the modest metropolis was no different from any other in the north of Italy. Wide straight avenues, first built by the Romans or even earlier, penetrated into the centre from each of the major points of the compass. Unloved high-rise buildings overlooked smaller petrol stations that bordered the roadside as tired trees failed to brighten the surroundings. But then each of these uninspiring thoroughfares ended at the ring road that enclosed the centre of the city, a circular road that ringed a bubble of protected antiquity within. Immediately inside the encircling road, a brilliant green swathe of sunken land stretched inward for a couple of hundred yards where a wide moat once lay. The verdant band was uninterrupted apart from at four points where it was punctuated by narrow lanes that branched off from the ring road and on through the dried up moat and beyond to the old city walls where archways allowed their progression through the ancient ramparts. The city walls were completely intact but that in itself was not an unusual feature in this grand old country. Less commonplace was their composition as the medieval stone structure was almost completely enveloped in a thick covering of turf. Only the wide top of the wall was exposed and paved to provide a promenade for joggers and meanders where armed soldiers would have peered down from centuries before.

Inside the city walls it was, to Laura, like stepping back in time. Traffic was limited to the very margins, creating a large pedestrainised area that brought an aura of calm and a lack of urgency to the streets and buildings. It was a picture postcard city, preserved yet alive with people and life and eccentricity, a place where art flourished in its many forms. Modern installations and sculptures were positioned on street corners, clashing but somehow fitting in with the venerable buildings that looked down upon them. Music drifted through the streets like leaves on the breeze, the deep rumble of a saxophone and the strident tinkling of a piano mingling harmoniously without having to compete with the din of traffic.

As a young teenager Laura would wander these very streets, soaking up the atmosphere and being drawn, like so many others, to the very core of this place. Here Laura would stare upon the impossibly brilliant whiteness of the church in Piazza san Michele or relax in the Piazza Napoleone where the neat lines of trees around the perimeter of the dirt-covered square made the scene more reminiscent of a Paris suburb than Tuscany.

Laura quickly fell in love with her idyllic surroundings and in time, when she was sixteen years of age, she also lost her heart to one of its inhabitants. Alessio was the young recipient of her affections, a member of an aristocratic family who claimed he would be a prince if Tuscany became an independent state once again. This was obviously a highly unlikely event but this did not matter to Laura. In her head she had grown up like a princess in a fairytale world and now she had found her prince.

For months they were allowed to court together, albeit under the close scrutiny of both sets of parents. Their relationship blossomed as one of pure adoration as they explored each other's minds and yearned to explore each other's bodies. Sadly, after a few months, the courtship was cut short. The soap opera that Laura's father starred in was flagging in the ratings. It needed a dramatic storyline and that turned out to involve her father's character being fatally wounded in an accident involving a bicycle and a runaway pig. It was an inauspicious end that Laura would later learn had as much do with her father's demands for a pay-rise as the dwindling viewers.

26

Laura was heart-broken twice over. First that she would have to leave her first love Lucca and secondly her prince Alessio. In truth she *could* have stayed. Now at the age of seventeen she could have remained without her parents but she would have had nowhere to live and no means by which to support herself. Her prince was similarly distraught but could not help her either. Despite his noble family's ancient connections and 'titles' their wealth was largely material, tied up in the bricks and mortar of their stately home with a weighty annual repair bill. There was no way he could afford to support her. Besides, they were too young to elope without the consent of their parents and then the court. A tearful request was made to their guardians but it fell on deaf ears.

And so with immense reluctance Laura left with her parents to go to Rome where her father had picked up some roles in a few television adverts whilst he looked for a longer-term contract. Laura promised her prince that she would return whenever she could and urged him to visit her in the capital. She swore that in a short year or two, when Laura had finished her studies and Alessio had access to his trust fund, they would get married and be together forever in Lucca.

Laura awoke to the sound of waves gently crashing against the shore. As her senses regained their sharpness she realised the sound of the sea was actually people clapping in the auditorium around her. The soft ululation was already being accompanied by the more jarring knocks of cushioned seats being released from their loads and springing back into their reclined position as the gentry began to make their way to the exits.

She sighed. It was the end of the movie and she had slept through the whole thing, reliving her adolescent days as she had slumbered. Now over a decade later that 'prince' really was a distant memory. Over the interceding years they exchanged letters and shared phone calls but they rarely found the opportunity (or the funds) to be able to meet each other in person. Gradually the love and lust they felt for each other drained like energy from a battery until it was all spent with no hope of it being re-charged. Nobody was to blame, just the circumstances of life and the twists of fate. Alessio and his family had experienced a slow decline in fortune during that time due to some ill-advised business decisions by Alessio's father. The culmination was Alessio having to work in a local supermarket, stacking shelves to pay the bills, even his hefty trust fund exhausted to help the family financially afloat.

In the ten years since Laura moved to Rome, she had learned to become at first familiar with the very different city, then comfortable, then finally dependant. The innocent and naïve girl who loved the fairy-tale and slow-paced world of Lucca had grown up into a more realistic and savvy woman in the very real and fast-paced world of the Italian capital. One vestige of her earlier life remained though – a little bit of the princess she once dreamt she was stayed inside her, still praying that one day she would find her prince.

After the break-up of her first relationship with Alessio, many suitors followed, a list that grew lengthy for a while as her reputation as an eligible, sophisticated and beautiful spinster on the Rome social scene burgeoned. It was a scene she had been introduced to through her father who had once again found minor fame (if not fortune) with a role in a major sit-com. Laura was able to pick and chose who she wanted, when she wanted, to the frustration of the fashionable bachelors. One at a time they came and went, each liaison cut short by the now fickle young lady citing one of a myriad of deficiencies she always spotted. The first was a young executive who worked in the higher echelons of the car maker Ferrari. He was dispatched after ten months following a furious row when Laura claimed he was cheating on her when he made his frequent trips to America. Next to try their chances was a French viscount some fifteen years her senior. Despite being wowed by the trappings of life in a French castle overlooking vineyards and serene valleys, the age gap proved to be too much of a gulf to leap. Others followed, punctuated by brief periods of solitude where she attempted to gain some space to herself or try in vain to follow in her father's footsteps and develop a career in acting.

As the years passed, the queue of bachelors gradually dwindled as she approached her thirties. There were still interested parties but Laura was beginning to lose the privilege to choose. Increasingly the men were in control and they opted for younger counterparts. She had had hopes with her latest partner though. Philipo de Mercati, (another of noble blood, although somewhat diluted by the time it filled his veins) had, to date, lasted nearly two years in happy courtship with Laura. After waiting for everyone else to leave, Laura rose from her seat. As the last of the geriatrics hobbled through the foyer after collecting their expensive fur coats from the cloakroom she glanced at her watch, realizing she had just under ten minutes to make it home before her new favourite television programme started.

She rushed from the theatre to the adjacent road where her battered but trusty Fiat littered the affluent surroundings. Gathering the many folds of her skirt as she cantered, she avoided sullying the expensive material with fresh mud, circumventing the puddles with long strides like a drunken triple jumper. Bundling herself into the unlocked vehicle and revving the engine far higher than its optimal design tolerances, she pulled away from her illegal parking place, oblivious to the parking sticker on the windscreen. Laura also failed to spot the darkly liveried car with its lights turned off that followed her silently onto the main road.

Laura had learned to drive in the calm and refined surrounds of Lucca. However, it did not take long after her arrival in the Italian capital to discover that the sedate driving style she had been taught was not appropriate for these hectic streets. In Rome the normal rules of the road were metaphorically torn up and thrown out of the window. Here it was the 'unofficial' rules of the road that took clear precedence. For example, each lane on an urban street was not deemed to be one car width but two. Traffic lights were largely ignored so that a red light merely meant 'beware of traffic from all directions' as opposed to 'stop'. Car horns sounded almost without abatement so that every vehicle ensures all others are abundantly aware of their presence and location at all times. The end result is a swirling, noisy and colourful cacophony of metal and weaving pedestrians that flows as slowly as molasses in all directions through the city, the components somehow almost always sliding past each other without contact, despite space being at a premium and collisions and scrapes seemingly the far more likely outcome.

The fluid dynamics of such mechanical balletics could almost be compared to another famous but arguably more impressive Roman phenomenon. Most evenings in summer, just before nightfall, thousands upon thousands of starlings would take to the sky above the area surrounding the central Termini railway station. Together the dark birds would form a super-flock, flying together in perfect unison, wing-tips almost but never touching, the single entity contracting and pulsing like a black heart, constantly shifting its shape by elongating itself and then rapidly contracting to create an infinite number of twisting Mobius-like configurations, the ever varying patches of density and sparcity in three-dimensional synchrony to an unseen orchestral conductor. The performance always ends suddenly when a few of the birds leave the group by diving quickly to find their roost for the night in one of the many surrounding trees. Eventually all follow, funnelling down from the top branches as rapidly as wine pouring from a carafe. After some initial jostling for position on the crowded boughs, the birds remain there to rest and to roost, perfectly calm until the morning.

It was calm now for Laura too as she sped along the now deserted roads in the evening darkness. Turning right she bounced her aged car along the poorly maintained highway that bordered the grand river Tiber and weaved past the large mosque, a building that always appeared so aesthetically out of place in this most classically Italian of suburban settings. Abandoning the flat valley floor she took the high road, houses now blocking the view of the river as the affluence of the neighbourhood visibly improved with altitude.

Looking in front of her to navigate her way through the narrowing streets, Laura never saw or heard the darkened car until it hit her from behind, smashing the rear light and sending her into a violent swerve that she only just managed to control, just avoiding being slammed into a looming roadside wall. Cursing, but suspecting poor driving rather than malice, she continued her journey, knowing that to stop and assess the damage in these dark deserted streets would put her at unnecessary risk, despite this being a prosperous quarter.

Through the rear view mirror, Laura could see the vehicle that had shunted her little Fiat, a huge dark car that had now retreated some distance back. She could not see the driver, silhouetted in the weak street lights. Maybe she had watched too many action films in her life but fear now gripped her chest like a vice as she felt sure that she was being followed. Instantly her survival instincts took over. She needed to lose her would-be assailant before he had another chance to ram her flimsy hatchback. Using her local knowledge she spun the car down a side street, one wheel leaving the ground momentarily before making contact again with a squeak of squealing rubber. Her pursuer, seemingly surprised by the sudden change in direction, only just managed to make the sharp turn, sparks flying as its bodywork scraped along stone walls before careering back into the centre of the narrow, high-walled alleyway. A cat scrambled out of the way just as the two cars rumbled past in quick succession, sending discarded sheets of newspaper and cardboard spiralling into the air. The bigger and more powerful car was now closing in, the distance to Laura's back bumper negligible as the driver readied himself for another menacing shove. Laura could now see the other end of the channelled alley up ahead and the sphincter that led to a wider street.

Out popped the Fiat, into the main road like a cork from a bottle, only one wing mirror being left behind in the deceptive bottleneck. Not sensing the danger, the larger car continued but came to an abrupt halt, wedged in the narrowing culvert with a shower of sparks and a deafening cacophony of crunching metal.

Seeing the car trapped made Laura laugh from relief as she forced herself to calm down despite adrenaline continuing to course through her body. She continued to drive home, a short journey from where she now was and parked her car haphazardly outside her apartment. Hurriedly she removed her stilettos and ran across the cobbles of the communal driveway, her hands shaking as she forced the key in the lock of her front door. Only once safely inside, with the door firmly locked and bolted behind her, did Laura take stock of what had just happened. Sat on the floor with her back slumped against the door, questions began to pepper her thoughts.

Laura had no idea why she was being chased. She had no enemies to her knowledge, no one with an axe to grind. Could it be a spurned ex-lover? There were plenty of them but she thought it unlikely any would resort to such violence. Could it even have been a case of mistaken identity or simply a case of road rage after she unknowingly cut someone up on her way home?

Suddenly her fear returned as she wondered if she was safe here in her flat. Stirred into action, Laura rushed through the apartment, checking that all the windows were locked, pulling the curtains tight across them. Glancing up at the burglar alarm she saw it was still blinking reassuringly. She knew she should call the police but not before she pulled herself a stiff drink to calm her nerves.

A generous gulp of neat Amaro Montenegro bitters scorched its way down her insides, burning through some of the knots in her muscles as it descended. It was only on the second swallow that Laura became aware that the television was on in her flat. She had set it to turn itself on automatically when a certain program started. It was a stupid reality show, the type that she would normally avoid but this particular televisual trash starred her fiancé Philipo as one of the contestants.

The show was based around a ridiculous concept but one that had most of the nation gripped. The contestants had been blindfolded and placed on a plane. After landing several hours later they were escorted onto a boat that sped them to a desert island in the middle of the ocean. (In reality they had been placed in a flight simulator and then taken to a small island off the coast of southern Italy. All facts of which the viewing audience were fully aware.)

Settling herself in front of tonight's fifty-third episode of "Island Tribes", Laura tried to regain some normality to her day. It had been strange at first seeing her lover every evening on her TV screen but she quickly got used to the experience. Once again she welled with pride and love as the daily highlights package today showed how her betrothed effortlessly settled an argument about coconut rations before bravely spearing a wild pig for dinner whist ignoring the flirtatious advances of two young waifs who vied for his attentions.

The scene then changed to later in the day and what was shown next resulted in the pride and adoration Laura felt quickly dissolving into anger and sorrow. Thinking he was safe from the cameras, Philipo was getting intimately acquainted with one of the more glamorous female contestants, (a former Miss Verona). A secret camera hidden in an over-hanging palm tree followed their amorous fumblings as they walked awkwardly together in a fervent embrace before they disappeared out of sight, underneath one of the provided bivouacs.

Everyone on the show and those that watched the show knew Phillipo was betrothed to Laura and therefore she was now being made a fool of in front of millions of people. Incandescent with rage, Laura took immediate action, turning out the contents of her Armani handbag (a gift from Philipo that would now have to go, along with many other things) and proceeded to hastily roll a spliff with shaking fingers. As the dense light grey smoke wafted away from her, so the fog of anger lifted in her head. Looking around at the scattered contents of her bag she saw something shiny she did not recognize. Like a magpie she picked it up. It was the sticker someone had pasted onto the back of her film invitation from that evening. The sticker appeared to be another invitation in itself.

The next morning Laura left her abode as she did every weekday morning. However, at the end of her road she turned left towards central Rome instead of right towards her office. Back at her apartment, her cat was already greedily eating the food that had been left in the automatic dispenser that also contained sustenance for the next two weeks under its other opaque time-locked segments. In the bedroom she had left rather a mess. Philipo's tailor–made and designer clothes were strewn across the floor, now worthless with countless rips and tears.

As Laura made her way her way to the destination printed neatly on the silvery sticker, the local police were crawling over the car that had perused her with such determination the previous night. The tired officer in charge was puzzled as he examined the vehicle that was still jammed in the culverted road. The car was empty and yet it appeared there was no way the driver could have escaped unless he had passed through the solid wall. The policeman patted his chest pocket instinctively for the packet of cigarettes that was not there. He had given them up that very morning but he was beginning to think it may not have been a good day to quit.

"Ok. So where is the pontiff then? I assume you did the deed in his private chambers?" said the Camerlengo, suddenly feeling the need for haste.

The object of the pointed question immediately looked sheepish, feeling like a pupil facing an impatient headmaster. "Umm...I am afraid not my master. His excellence was enjoying a stroll in his gardens so we had to do it there."

The Camerlengo hesitated and narrowed his eyes. "That will make things a little messy. Never mind, what's done is done. Come with me and we'll go and do the necessary." The holy chamberlain whizzed past his servant and through the doorway without looking back. For the first time he felt a tinge of fear that something would go awry. He knew he had made all the required precautions but with so much that could go wrong there was always an inherent risk, however small. Ergo, as soon as the old fart was in a nailed down coffin the better.

The Camerlengo grimaced and hitched up his ankle length cloak as he tiptoed out into the gardens, following the unsure pointing arm of his grubby assistant. Ahead, at the entrance to the maze, two of the other Swiss guards who had got their hands dirty were standing guard. At the sight of the Camerlengo they slunk out of sight around the first corner of manicured hedgerow. The Camerlengo followed them around the side of the topiaried folly and all four men looked at the ground, surveying the murder scene.

"Great job lads. Only one problem...Where exactly is the pontiff's head?" the Camerlengo added.

The initial praise from their master had put the briefest of smiles on the faces of the dullards, a positive sign of emotion that evaporated when they simultaneously detected the intended sarcasm and the missing bonce.

The Camerlengo didn't wait for an answer. "For goodness sake just find the rest of him, bring him in and clean him up. We'll have to attach his head again somehow for the open casket before we can put him in the coffin." He angrily trudged off, leaving his partners in crime to peer under hedges for the missing body part. As the Camerlengo trudged back to his office he paused for only a moment to wipe some blood stained mud off his Gucci shoes.

Thirty minutes later the entire papal staff of the Vatican were assembled in the Pope's private quarters. Only a few souls were excused, mainly Swiss Guards who were responsible for security and manning the telephone switchboard. The household staff, some several hundred strong, were now crammed uneasily in the largest room in this inner sanctum of the Pope's meagre quarters.

The mood in the chamber was sombre, reflected by the heavy curtains that were drawn closed to block out the natural light from the numerous windows and the large gothic candles that had been lit and were strewn around the room. The flickering flames provided the only light giving a gloomy Baroque feel to the enclosed space. Nobody had been told why they had all been called but they all knew there were very few occasions that warranted such an ad hoc (but compulsory) attendance. They were aware that the death of their leader, their pope, was the most likely scenario as it was tradition that his staff would be granted an audience with the newly departed soul before any of the public were informed, allowing his employees time for a personal out-flowing of grief before the world could join them in collective lamentation.

The Pope had not been unwell but he was of very advanced years and it would not be a surprise for an elderly gentleman such as him to be struck down by some quick, fatal stroke or perhaps a heart attack. Of course none would have dared suspect that it was a 'quick stroke' of a rather different kind, not delivered by God (as was the ancient explanation for such a mental affliction) but one of their very own staff through the medium of a sturdy hammer.

Everyone had been waiting patiently for some minutes when their worst fears were confirmed. The open coffin of the now deceased pontiff glided into view, the casket being wheeled in by the Camerlengo and his assistants, the means of propulsion covered by an ornate purple velvety gown. Some gasped and others began to weep openly, the noise of grief concealing a squeaking wheel in need of lubrication.

The Camerlengo frowned again at his assistants who purposely averted his fierce gaze as they all helped to push the dead Pope in front of his adoring audience. He had told the nincompoops to find a graceful way of transporting the dead body into the room and the best they could do was a rickety aluminium electrically heated hostess trolley draped with the Pope's very own bed cover. The pope's assistant stifled a yelp of pain as he stepped on the pins of the trailing plug for the third time. At least, he thought, the low lighting made the carriage look far more grand than it actually was.

Of course the Camerlengo knew it was protocol for the coffin to be carried gracefully into the room on the shoulders of the Camerlengo and three of his assistants, one at each corner of the coffin. He had no intention of lifting that heavyweight cadaver above his head though. It would almost certainly put his back into spasm again, a spine weakened by years of literally bending over backwards for the ungrateful sod. Besides, no one was going to argue with him on such a pedantic point at this time of sorrow and for now, in this period of papal vacancy (the *sede vacante*), he was in charge of everything that happened with the two miles of impregnable walls that contained the 110 acres of the Vatican city.

Putting his thoughts of power aside for one moment, the Camerlengo brought the wheeled table to a halt at the front of the room, his assistants obediently stepping out of the way. The Pope's confidante then duly started the one stupid ritual that sadly could not be avoided. It was largely symbolic but verifying the death of the pope was always expected. At least the trust afforded him in this role meant that his immoral plans had only been possible due to another convention surrounding the death of any pope – a proper post mortem was always forbidden.

The Camerlengo stood behind the coffin so that the assembled patrons could see both himself and the coffin. He began the ritual by raising the limp left hand of the corpse and gently removing the ceremonial *Ring of the Fishermen* from the Pope's hand, the action symbolizing the end of the Pope's reign. With a pair of secateurs he grasped the ring and cut it in half with a metallic 'clink' that made the people in the front row jump at the sudden sound. Next, from a pocket in his cloak, he produced a small silver hammer. Following the ancient instructions he brought the mallet down to strike the Pope's head, simultaneously calling out "*Vincenzo dormisne?*" (Vincenzo, are you sleeping?). Twice he repeated the question but unfortunately on the third strike of the hammer he unintentionally used a little too much force, causing the hastily reattached head to depart once more from its body with a sickening sound. Free from its hastily wrought attachments fashioned from sticky tape, it rolled to the edge of the velveteen-covered trolley, falling to the floor despite a despairing lunge from The Camerlengo. The small hammer he had released in haste (in order to leap for the falling head) flew through the air before making contact with the forehead of his nearest assistant, knocking him out cold before he toppled onto the decapitated pontiff's rotund abdomen.

I-VI – BOLOGNA

Alice was in a hurry, a normal state of being for someone like her who used a frantic pace of life to occupy her mind and stop her thoughts wandering to unwanted destinations. However the commodity of time was especially at a premium at that moment and the evening rush hour in the centre of Bologna was therefore a hindrance. Even though it was nearly 8pm, the clogging vehicles were still slowly filtering out from the ancient centre to the circumventing ring road and beyond, like lumpy flour shaken through a sieve. This stationary traffic did not unduly impede Alice's progress although she lost valuable time having to weave around the metal boxes that crammed the labyrinthine roadways of the city on her battered Vespa scooter. Barely slowing as she turned onto a cobbled street, the almost bald tyres squeaked on the slippery surface as they struggled to maintain a purchase. An elderly pedestrian was in her way but the old woman merely waddled on with her shopping, all too used to the younger generation carelessly careering through the streets on their motorized scooters.

Drifting around one more corner she was at last home, screeching to a halt outside the non-descript building. Alice leapt off her bike, athletically removing her helmet at the same time, her tightly coiled flaxen and auburn locks springing out in all directions like an explosion in a bedspring factory. She jumped up onto the slightly raised platform of the colonnade as she fished the door keys from her bag. In an instant, she was through the front door and racing up the stone stairs to her third floor flat, her hair following her, the tendrils dragged reluctantly against their will. Leaping two steps at a time, the wiry thirty-year-old soared past the potted ferns that she never noticed. Ferns that were strategically placed to break up the monotonous cream décor and cared for by a neighbour she had never met.

Flying through the apartment like a hungry eagle looking for prey, Alice looked for anything out of place and quickly found something, slamming shut a window in a pique of anger. A window that her *coinquilino*, her housemate, had left open since he had skulked out that morning. In truth he was more of a tenant than a 'mate' as she had no time or desire to get to know him. Satisfied that the grubby male who shared her personal space had not left his mark elsewhere, she hurled herself up the steep wooden ladder that allowed access to her cramped but quaint bedroom that was once the loft space.

Alice did not have time to stare out of the small slanted window at the building across the road but she could not help herself at that moment as she saw the students of the evening dance class begin their warm-up exercises. She could see herself in the eager but clumsy faces belonging to those who willed their limbs to perform ever more complex balletic feats. Alice peeled her eyes away from the movements of the aspiring adolescents and undressed, placing her clothes neatly on her bedside chair.

Her bed was in reality nothing more than a shallow mattress resting on wooden slats as there was room for little more in the small and low-ceilinged boudoir. Above the bed a birdcage hung from the wall with a stuffed bird inside, a once vibrant finch, now greying and glued to its perch. Against the opposite wall, a grand cocktail cabinet stood, housing various haphazardly arranged bottles of liquors and mixers. A thick layer of dust shrouded them all, fogging the visual effect of a kaleidoscope of coloured labels that had partially peeled and cracked with age. Behind the bed on the back wall, happy memories of innocence and hope stared through time from the past to the present. The sparkle still burned bright through the eyes that looked confidently straight into the camera. Eyes that opened into the souls of a much younger Alice and her childhood friends, often pictured straight after they had finished a dance production, the sweat of exertion still glistening on rosy round adolescent cheeks, strongly lit by the powerful theatre lights.

Then as now the dream was the same. But then she had time and youth on her side, they all had. Now Alice was thirty she was considered over the hill as far as her chosen career path was concerned. All her friends had given up their dreams years ago, some choosing the easy option of a dreary office job or, if their parents could afford it, continuing their education to gain as many qualifications as possible and aim for a better-paid job in a country where unemployment was constantly high and the prospects low.

The rest of Alice's flat was furnished in an attempt to create a relaxing atmosphere of idyllic home life. The result however was a little too static, staid and old fashioned. A new visitor would not see a snapshot of happy home life but rather a staged, department store image of how a living space *should* be, filled by the prerequisite object d'art. One ethereal centrepiece was missing though, that "lived-in" feel. Maybe it was that the two dining chairs were a little two neatly arranged at each end of the small table that was pushed out of the way by the window instead of in the centre of the room. Or perhaps the delicate lace runner was placed a little too symmetrically through the centre of that forgotten table. Even the books housed in the shelving by the front door were aligned with more than a hint of obsessive compulsion, giving the impression of flimsy plastic fakes rather than the solid tomes they actually were. The small galley kitchen completed the feel of a residence used infrequently for anything other than sleeping, with cupboards so empty that not even a mouse would be enticed to linger and a bowl of shrinking, wrinkling apples on the worktop.

Alice had just returned from an audition in Milan that day, a trip that was the main reason for both her current anger and tardiness. She had travelled north west to the fashion capital of Italy in good spirits. The invitee who had called the previous week had been full of praise for her previous work and seemed to all but confirm that there would be a place for her in the show. It was an exciting new production that was going to start in Milan before touring Europe. There was even the possibility of a tour to the U.S. if the European leg went well. Alice dared to dream of working and even living in America as it was the very pinnacle of her dream. How she yearned to tread the boards of sophisticated Broadway or even make a career as a dancer in Hollywood films. Earlier, on the train to Milan, hope and adrenalin had flowed through her, positive spirits even spreading to some of the other normally dour passengers who mirrored her smile when she happened to look in their direction. Against her better judgment and years of bitter experiences she had banished all the possible negative outcomes to the back of her mind. Surely this time it would be her big break?

The audition went well, she could feel it and sense it in the faces and the body language of the three well-dressed judges sat in the front rows of the empty theatre. As her small lycra-covered frame heaved from the after effects of physical exertion and the thrill of anticipation the judges quietly conversed, consulting notes and nodding heads. Finally the middle judge pressed the button on the desk in front of him to activate the loudspeaker. (Despite being easily near enough to make himself heard if he raised his voice, the man with Alice's future in his hands obviously felt such a base ululation was beneath him). He began to speak, Alice shielding the blinding lights with her hand so she could see his impassive face. They man coldly stated that all the judges were delighted with her performance and they would certainly have liked to choose her for the role, the leading role in fact…if only she had been younger. Alice's face dropped almost as far as the well-trod boards. They said they would obviously keep her details and as soon as they had a role for a more 'mature' performer such as herself they would call her straight back. Retaining her composure, Alice kept her interior feelings from her exterior until she had taken her 'aged' body off the stage and out of sight of the panellists, taking her frustration out on the nearest backstage door with a swift roundhouse kick.

She should have guessed it was all too good to be true. This was all too common in a country were ability meant nothing if you were over thirty and female. She was not going to hold her breath and sit by the phone as in all probability it was not going to ring, not from that company anyway. For Alice it would be back to the day job tomorrow (or to be more accurate the night job) in the slightly seedy cocktail bar and dance club in a less than salubrious suburb of Bologna. She had one more appointment in a couple of days in the Vatican of all places but she was not sure that would amount to anything, the invite she had received had seemed genuine but the venue was just so unlikely. Still, beggars could not be choosers, especially 'old' beggars like herself.

Alice tried to wash away the troubles of her day with a quick shower, tying her hair back so that it would not get wet and make her lose an hour drying it. Towelling herself dry without due care and attention she selected just one item of clothing, a pre-ironed dress that was hanging and ready to wear in her large wardrobe. Her last actions before leaving the unloved abode were to swing a battered jacket over her slender shoulders, grab a wrinkled apple from the bowl in one hand and her shoes in the other.

Mari had a love/hate relationship with birthdays. She loved the attention from her family and friends but resented the extra year added to her age, seemingly in one fell swoop instead of a day at a time. She sat in the Irish bar talking about everything and nothing as she and her friends awaited the last tardy arrival. Not that Mari was talking with her friends – as usual she was on her phone, loudly discussing furnishings with a client who wanted the interior of his summer house in Ravenna completely redesigned. It was after 8pm but as far as she was concerned any waking hour was a potential business hour. Finally she finished the call, snapping the flip phone shut with unnecessary force. Almost instantly she opened her mobile again to check for any messages before she tentatively placed the bright red phone in her red bag that matched her red skirt. (Patiently waiting at home in a drawer for the right occasion were four identical phones in blue, black, green and pink). Mari stared at each friend in turn, trying to pick up the thread of conversation she had been missing. Deciding the topic was not that interesting, she reached into her bag again to retrieve her phone and proceeded to send a text to a friend bemoaning the choice of the Irish Bar for drinks. (If she had known the choice of venue in advance she obviously would have worn green and not red).

Mari hadn't always disliked the Irish bar. As teenagers they had all loved to spend time at *Clauricane*. On Sunday afternoons they would excuse themselves early from family lunches to while away the hours in the dark, smoky confines by playing pool, chatting to older boys and generally feeling more grown up than they actually were. At the time, it was seen as a new and novel place to go and hang out. Before the 1980's, places to drink in Italy were generally small and a place for old men wearing hats and sporting moustaches to animatedly discuss the finer points of football and politics. They were certainly not a place for loud youngsters. Therefore *Clauricane* was a revelation when it first opened its wide swinging doors on *via Zamboni*, in a sweet spot between the centre and the university. Here the old rules of Italian drinking establishments were disobediently ignored. The interior was uncluttered and spacious with a scattering of tables and even sofas, not the traditional small room filled with regimented lines of uncomfortable stools. Patriotic beers like *Peroni* and *Moretti* were absent, fashionable sounding lagers from the United Kingdom and Ireland taking their place. The walls and ceilings were not covered in mirrors and football paraphernalia but were adorned with 'authentic' Irish signposts, posters and even the odd musical instrument. As well as drawing in the local adolescents, it also rapidly gained a reputation as a *Mecca* for university students who were schooled just a stumbling distance along the road. To Mari and her young friends it had felt as though all the young people of the world had been brought to their doorstep through the magic portal of the Irish Bar. Today though the Irish Bar was far from unique and just one of many similar establishments dotted around the city, some of which even adopted an 'authentic' Scottish or Welsh theme. The novelty may had worn off many years ago but it was still a good place to drink that brought back pleasant memories of their well spent youth.

Elena glanced at her watch and realized that she should really stop chatting and head back home. She had only intended to pop in to meet everyone for a quick drink after work, knowing she could not stay long as she would have to rush home to take her dog Alfred for a walk. She bit her lip guiltily, guessing that by now the virtually uncontrollable Great Dane would be bouncing around the house in anticipation of the return of her owner, reacting to every sound in the hope it was is owner's keys at the front door. He was barely more than a puppy but already stood well past her knees. She was well aware she shouldn't let him have the run of the apartment - he had already ruined the sofa and destroyed a couple of expensive vases - but having him cooped up in one room only concentrated his boundless (and destructive energies). Elena would come back and re-join the party later. All her friends had grown to understand that her dog was the most important thing in her life after her family. In fact, in truth he *was* part of her family.

As Elena left, promising to return within an hour, Veronica arrived, the two friends embracing briefly in the doorway, the new entrant practically still glowing after she had arrived directly after one of her frequent visits to the tanning salon. Naturally dark-skinned, she was intent on emphasising her mahogany tones at every opportunity. Ideally this would be achieved naturally by jetting off to hot climates but her hectic social calendar and other more tedious commitments meant she often had to rely on the short bursts of ultra-violet rays provided by the local solarium. At least a monthly allowance from her wealthy parents enabled her to not have to consider finding a job and gave her the time she required to indulge in such 'essential' treatments. Now in her thirties and finally breaking free from the bosom of her family abode, Veronica resided in an apartment in the part of town that was considered to be the 'place to be'. It was pure coincidence, she told herself, that the building was less than a kilometre from her parent's house.

Finally Alice swept through the door to the small bar as if striding on a catwalk. She barely acknowledged the waving arms and smiling faces of her friends as she made a bee-line for the bar to order a half pint of Tennants Super, whilst still clutching the wrinkled apple she had brought from home. The friends made space for the late arrival around the inadequately small table and conversations reignited as she gulped down the strong lager. She disliked the metallic aftertaste but, as many Italians, she viewed the beer as a deluxe exported beer and liked the strong 'pick-me-up' after a long day.

The group grazed slowly on the delicious morsels of food provided for those patrons who bought drinks during this *apperitivo* period (apart from Alice who munched on her apple) as plans were made for a much later dinner at a local *osteria*. They shared their experiences of the day, the week and current gossip both local and worldwide, the words fired passionately from their mouths like gunfire. Some of the verbal bullets hit home, eliciting wounds of shock from the recipient whereas others were rebounded with a dismissive hand or a shrug.

On the face of it the topics of conversation had not changed much in the years and even decades they had all known each other but as time and birthdays slipped by the spectres of words unsaid loomed larger in the corner of each of their mind's eye. They were four independent and confident women, approaching thirty (or just beyond) but none knew what the future was to hold in terms of careers or significant others. There was still time, they all told themselves secretly. Time before they had to find love or a job they actually enjoyed. Besides, for some of them these desires did not burn strong within.

Elena had just returned to her apartment from walking Alfred, although in truth it was more a case of the dog leading the owner. As Alfred padded about the apartment, content that he had reasserted his authority, Elena quickly filled a mug of water and drank half before stepping onto her balcony to quench the thirst of her limp chilli plants that had clearly suffered in the earlier daytime heat. Absently she watered the frazzled dark green leafy stalks, allowing her gaze to lift to the dusk sky. To the south and west she could just make out the old church of *San Luca* on the hill above the city, sitting proud like a lizard basking in the last few rays of sunshine, the light bouncing off the old walls with a soft radiance.

For a moment her view was partially obscured by something that fell in front of the church and rolled away, following the gradient of the hillside down the snaking road that led to the affluent suburbs on the southern edge of Bologna, the object then disappearing out of view behind a screen of trees. A few seconds past before the same thing happened again. Elena became transfixed, squinting and even leaning slightly forward over the balcony in an attempt to discern what was occurring in the fading light some three miles away. Somehow Alfred became aware of the strange happening from inside the apartment. Elena heard the unmistakable sound of unclipped canine toenails scrabbling for grip on the smooth floor before he cantered out to join her, barking in the direction of the church.

Only fifteen seconds had passed but three shapes had already fallen to the ground. It was at that point when the first sound hit Elena's ears, followed five seconds later by the next and the next. The sound was an almighty boom, not unlike the rumble at the end of a thunderclap or a sonic boom as a jumbo jet punctured the sound barrier. For over a minute further objects continued to fall and roll out of sight.

Although she could not see exactly what these things were or from where they had originated, Elena sensed something out of ordinary was going on and that the residents of the city were in danger if they were unfortunate enough to be in the path of these curiosities. Most importantly to her, those residents included her friends who perhaps sat unaware in the Irish pub or unprotected through the streets on the way to the restaurant.

She tried to call the emergency services but the number was unobtainable. She tried to call her friends. No signal. Without wasting any more time she left Alfred, barking on the balcony and skidded out of her front door, flying down the six flights of stairs, knowing it would be quicker than waiting for the ancient caged lift to drag itself up to her floor and down to street level again. Hurling her slight frame onto the even slighter frame of her old bicycle she tore up the streets, long hair straining to be free against its ties. (Luckily she never kept the bike locked up as she rightly assumed nobody would bother to steal such a decrepit machine). Taking the most direct route, Elena hared the wrong way down one-way streets and other avenues reserved for pedestrians. She found little resistance at this time of the evening apart from a guilty looking man in a suit who had to spin out of the way as he attempted to protect a bouquet of flowers destined for his long-suffering wife.

Elsewhere in the city, many locals stopped what they were doing as they saw the shapes first hand. Even the famously stubborn old ladies who sat outside their small houses abandoned hand-making their richly yellow fresh tortellini for the ragu that evening as up close, the terrified witnesses saw huge roughly hewn boulders, looming higher than two men as they careered down the hillside road. With immense force and momentum fuelled by gravity, the giant spheres of reddish stone leapt and bounced along, denting the soft tarmac, each heavy impact jettisoning smaller stones ricocheting off all directions. At times the great balls would collide with each other, sending each immense sphere off to either side of the road where they would rebound off the high grass bank with a dull thud. In places the earthen barrier would drop down temporarily to accommodate roadside buildings. Those houses unfortunate enough to be in the path of one of these destructive balls of rock paid the price with shattered windows and lintels.

As if drawn like metal marbles to a magnet, the boulders would not be stopped by anything and continued to the bottom of the hill at a pace where their first true obstacle loomed in the form of a crossroads patrolled by automatic traffic lights. A red light shone but the boulders paid no heed, flattening two of the signals with disdain before crushing the bonnets of two cars that dared to get in the way. The narrowing road did stop one of the deadly stones though, an untimely bounce off a curb sending it spinning into a ice-cream parlour on the corner of the intersection, leaving the remaining boulders to plough on through the darkening streets.

Startled pedestrians dived into doorways to seek refuge or pinned themselves against the walls, hoping the giant rocks would bounce harmlessly past. Miraculously nobody was crushed as the spheres continued on their destructive path, their speed somehow being maintained on the flat ground as if powered by an unseen force. On they ploughed, now just a couple of streets away from the historic city centre and its wide open piazza.

Elena burst out of the last narrow side street and into the wide boulevard of *via Ugo Bassi*, the main street that ran west to east through the heart of the city centre. Taking the shortest route, she pedalled furiously along the narrow pavement, again drawing frowned looks and cursed expletives from the assorted perambulators who had to take evasive action to avoid her clanking bicycle. She allowed herself a relieved, almost manic smile. Her limbs were aching but she had almost made it. She was sure she would have time to warn her friends and others from this bizarre menace. Half way down the street she turned a sharp right after the main library and into the main piazza. Skirting the railings used to prevent cars and motorbikes from using the area as a car park, she rounded Neptune's statue and into the square. There she stopped suddenly using a combination of poor brakes and good shoe leather. She could not see her friends yet but she knew they would pass this way on the way to their favourite restaurant. She scanned the vast expanse in front of her, trying to remember what they were wearing and fruitlessly honing in on one group of people after another. It was not going to be an easy task to locate her friends as the square was crowded with people.

Many people were sitting on plastic chairs that filled half the square, all arranged in regimented rows as they awaited the start of the film that was about to be shown on the outdoor screen. Others were walking slowly around the perimeter, climbing the steps that bordered the north side to peruse the menu of the expensive restaurant that straddled its length. Some diners here were already seated, surrounded by waiters who buzzed like flies between the tables.

Elena knew she should warn everyone here and not just her friends but she also knew they would not believe her, only her friends would trust her tall tale in time. At last she spied them sauntering into the quadrangle from the opposite corner, even at a distance Alice's tell-tale bouncing curly tendrils were unmistakable. Elena tried to attract their attention by desperately waving her arms. It caught the attention of many people nearby who looked on quizzically but her acquaintances did not see her through the deepening crowd. In the distance she could now start to hear the strain of a siren, several sirens in fact. Help would be on its way to stop the runaway boulders, she thought.

Elena thought about shouting over the heads of the masses to Alice and the others but she knew she would not be heard from so far away. She had to get nearer. Pumping her pedals once more she propelled her rusty steed towards Alice and the others, weaving skilfully around couples, children and old women. Finally her friends saw her and stopped in their tracks, puzzled and amused by the sight of their hectic friend whose movements were normally so measured and lady-like. Elena caught their collective gaze just in time as she could see what they could not – the first of the boulders arcing from behind them on a collision course with the unknowing troupe. She had just enough time to point up into the sky above the rooftops behind them, the others playing along and turning to where her finger indicated. Only then could they see for themselves just why she had been in such a rush.

In a heartbeat everyone in the piazza was staring at where Elena had been pointing. A moment of quiet hesitation and bewilderment was followed by bedlam. People scattered in every direction like ants seeking refuge from a sudden rainstorm. After what seemed like an age the boulder came down to earth, mercifully missing the small scurrying shapes with its first booming bounce that sent the projectile towards the huge fabric cinema screen, bursting through as if the strong material was made of paper. The second bounce sprayed chairs in a curving wave, broken legs spiralling away like matchsticks. Finally it came to rest harmlessly against the fountain of Neptune, its momentum finally ceased by the God of the sea that was now darkening the rough shape with water from its many spouts.

Before anyone could relax, a second boulder entered the scene, rolling from around a corner and veering along the enclosed promenade outside the restaurant, crushing tables, wine bottles and plates beneath its great bulk. It too harmlessly continued on and out into the main high street where if finally ran out of steam against the famous twin stone towers, a bowling ball that failed to knock down its skittles. The last three giant rocks loomed over the now almost empty piazza. Nearly all the occupants had found safe refuge in nearby buildings. Others chose to keep running, their flight response more sensitive than others.

In the open space of the square, only Alice and her friends remained, Elena still saddled on her bike. They had been unable to make their escape as the remaining boulders had somehow curved around them and hemmed them in and now headed directly for them as a fearsome bounding trio. All of the young women were frozen to the spot with fear except for Alice. She ran towards the giant rocks before launching her lithe form acrobatically into the air. Making a glancing contact with the outer-most boulder of the trio she then sprang to the side, landing like a cat. Her collision with the rock was subtle but enough to change the trajectory of the sphere so that it veered away from her friends, cannoning into the other two giant stones, the combined force of the billiard shot splitting all of the rocks asunder, the resultant rubble spraying across the piazza. As her friends rushed over to applaud her acrobatics and bravery that had saved their lives, Alice herself was still in shock, partly at the agility that had enabled her to stop the giant rolling weights but also at how the inanimate objects appeared to be sentient and mortally attracted to her.

I-VII – VATICANO

The Camerlengo and his assistants froze as stiff the Pope's rigor mortis stricken corpse. Two of them stared at the congregation, fearing their reaction to the pope losing his head, whereas the third member of their group laid prostate on the floor after being knocked out by the ceremonial hammer, mirroring the pontiff's horizontal pose. The Camerlengo scanned the room in panic but incredibly nobody had seemed to notice the unintended papal decapitation! Perhaps the dimly lit room concealed the horror of what had just happened to the onlookers or maybe because everyone was now bowed in prayer with their eyes firmly shut. Whatever the reason, the Camerlengo gathered his senses, not wanting to test his good fortune further by continuing his hesitation. Wiping his brow he swiftly moved around to the front of the trolley, pretending to pray as he replaced the head, covering the severed neck with a loop of the velveteen covering. Rousing his one alert colleague, together they began to wheel the body out of the room, solemnly nodding to the respectful crowd as they practically rushed through the doors, many pairs of tearful eyes now following them to catch one last glimpse of the kindly old pope.

Safely back at his desk after dispatching his bumbling assistants, the Camerlengo took time to think. There was still much to do in a short space of time but every step and every action had been rehearsed in his head a thousand times or more. *Io sono pronto.* I am ready, he said to himself.

First on the list of tasks to complete before he could claim his ultimate prize was the Pope's funeral. This was a straight forward affair with protocols and orders of events that would be taken care of by other less senior officials from within the papal state. All that was required of the late Pope's assistant was to sign a couple of key documents to set the funereal ball rolling. In his view this was a boring event that he would try to hasten before the next far more tantalizing task - the conclave that would chose the new Pope. This he was looking forward to as he was required to oversee the elaborate voting process in every last detail.

He smirked at the ingenuity and daring of his master plan. It was so simple and brilliant but could only be achieved in such a place as The Vatican, a sovereign state, housed in a fortress and protected by a private, independent army, cut off from the outside world. It was its undeniable strength but also its fatal weakness and a weakness the Camerlengo was about to fully exploit.

Dino Capelli looked out of place as he slouched in a chair outside the famous Café Gambrinus in the heart of Naples. Despite drinking its trademark *Professore* coffee, the young man in his last flush of youth looked scruffy compared to the other patrons sitting outside the salubrious establishment, unaware of the looks from the affluent older gentlemen who perched uncomfortably nearby, frowning at his dusty and ripped attire. Their disdain was soon reallocated however as a rowdy babble of middle-aged American tourists arrived, their gaudy garb barely covering protruding bellies suffixed by protruding camera lenses that settled around their spherical waists. The local elders sighed, wishing *The Talented Mister Ripley* had never been made, turning their exclusive establishment into a down-market and fabricated tourist attraction almost overnight.

Ignoring the embarrassingly thick froth on his upper lip from the creamy beverage, Dino could feel the restorative powers of the caffeine and sugar rich coffee reinvigorating his battered limbs. If only it could do the same for his suit that had not fared well during the tumble down Mount Vesuvius an hour or so previously.

A few hours before this moment, Dino had been leading a small group of tourists up the slopes of the slumbering volcano. All had been going well until they reached the top. There at the summit his mischievous over-exuberance got the better of him as one careless slip of the tongue caused his clients to suspect his credentials were not quite what they appeared to be (despite his official looking name badge and clip-board) and to a man they demanded their (not insignificant) fees to be returned forthwith. Unfortunately for his disgruntled patrons, Dino had already mentally earmarked his newly-acquired bounty achieved by subtle deception and was reluctant to return the wad of cash. Therefore, rather than acquiescing to their vehement request, Dino decided he would rather keep his ill-gotten gains and made a hasty retreat directly down the side of the mountain, closely followed by two of the misguided group, a disconcertingly fast and muscular duo. Despite the wrath of their lost Euros driving them on, the irked pair could not gain on the fleet-footed local, a misspent youth (and young adulthood) giving him the ability to flee any scene regardless of the terrain, or so he thought. Half way down the steep slope, the loose scree of the mountainside proved literally to be his downfall, his leading foot suddenly losing its precarious grip, sending the fake tour guide into an uncontrolled rolling tumble towards the tree line. His speed was now faster than any man would dare to run on the unstable surface and his pursuers were left to shake their fists in anger as their quarry bounded out of sight way below them. The joy of victory would have to be savoured later for Dino though as he unnervingly sought all the most pointed rocks on his descent. Finally he came to rest against a spruce sapling as the lower, more shallow slopes allowed the small fir trees to eke out an existence on the stony incline. As Dino counted all his limbs and appendages, he could not help but shake his head at his misfortune at finding the only intelligent Americans this side of Rome. Most tourists had been gullible enough to believe him when he said the interior of the volcano is now used by the former Italian president Berlusconi to hide fleet of private jets and helicopters!

At least a fervent check of his pockets after his tumbling escape had shown that only a few of the banknotes he had conned out of the Yanks had been lost to the hill-side. It had been another profitable scam that had kept him in fine wine and questionable women for a few weeks but it was time to move on. The cash he purloined today would keep him going for a while but he would need a new confidence trick to sustain his diversions before very long. As for the consequences from today's unfortunate event, he was sure to be reported to the local *polizia* but that was not a massive worry. They would describe a man in his late twenties or early thirties with shoulder length dark hair and a full moustache. With the eschewed wig and false moustache now grazing on the side of Vesuvius like small furry creatures he looked very different. Besides, there were thousands of men his age with dark hair in Naples. He knew it was unlikely he would ever be successfully identified and the tourists he duped would have lighter wallets but a story to tell their neighbours and work colleagues when they returned back home.

Painfully he limped the three kilometres back to a local train station on the *circumvesuviana*, the very earliest stretch of railway line in the whole of Italy. Today it was just a short branch line connected to the vast network that stretched thorough the country and underneath the alps to the rest of Europe, a tightrope over the precariously narrow ribbon of land between the sea on one side and the volcano on the other, the route connecting Naples with the tourist attractions of the ruins of Pompeii, Herculaneum and the nondescript modern suburbs that crowded around them. The occupants of the train that afternoon were the same as always, a mixture of locals like himself, (mainly dour tired faces going about their business) and the happy colourful tourists eager to see the historic sites, generally confused by the ugly and dusty high-rise buildings and endless looping suspended wires and cables they had to view en route.

Despite their differences, both groups uniformly afforded the dirty, ripped and slightly bloodied Dino a wide berth in that particular carriage. Ignoring them all, he slunk in the seat, legs wide apart, smirking to himself as they past the ancient site of Pompeii, remembering a previous incarnation as a guide there, another tenure prematurely curtailed. What tall tales he used to tell about that place, he recalled. But sometimes, ironically, it was the truths he told that people had not wanted to believe. Most people thought that the ruined city was discovered exactly as you see it today but in fact it had been rebuilt twice after it had originally been unearthed in the 18th century, once when it fell into disrepair and then again after being heavily bombed in the second world war. (The old bridge in Florence was too pretty for Hitler to destroy but it seemed Eisenhower did not think the old city at Pompeii shared the same aesthetic qualities.) Even those bodies preserved in ash are not exactly what they seem. Only cavities were found where the bodies once were and the famous casts are just where modern plaster was poured into the body-shaped holes. Several copies of the more 'appealing' stricken poses were even copied and now exist in museums around the world, the 'population' of that stricken town now represented as many times larger than the true number of souls that actually perished that fateful day in 79 AD.

Back to the present, and back in his native Napoli after the short train ride Dino stared absently across the pretty piazza situated in the throbbing heart of the city centre, here used as a busy road junction and not given over to pedestrians. (This was untypical for Italy but very typical for Naples where the automobile was the master of all that it purveyed). His gaze passed through one line of angry traffic to the small roundabout in the middle, marked by one of the main fountains in the city. This particular waterspout was more picturesque than most and was often used as a backdrop for wedding photos. Indeed as he mused, a wedding party dashed across the line of traffic, the bride hitching her skirt up and carrying her shoes as the whole party risked their lives just for a brief photo opportunity. The photographer wisely stayed safely outside the café, inconsiderately pushing tables back with his rear to obtain a better perspective. The bride, groom and immediate family struggled to interpret the instructions of the snapper over the din as children ran in circles around the pool that formed beneath the delicately carved statue, one small boy deciding to clumsily drink from the clear waters as his mother's back was turned, soaking his expensively-hired miniature suit in the process. It was at that moment that a new entrepreneurial notion sprang to Dino's mind. A small smile cracked open across his dusty face as he wondered whether this would be *the* scam that would finally make his fortune. With renewed vigour he rose from his chair, leaving his coffee half drunk, its restorative qualities no longer required. As he weaved through the carefully ordered chairs he could not help but mischievously nudge the photographer just as he pressed the button after minutes of waiting for a rare break in traffic.

Dino decided to return home to his apartment for an afternoon siesta. After all, one of the many benefits of being an entrepreneur meant he could work and sleep when he liked. It was a short walk of only a couple of hundred meters back to his pad from his favourite café but it was often an eventful one and that day proved to be no exception. Turning the corner from the Café Gambrinus, he faced the stark and businesslike building that housed the local dignitaries. Today it stood steadfast against the vociferous crowd that had gathered to protest against the faceless double-doors. Their vocal tirade was furnished with colourful banners, scrawled in thick black paint with the key points of their disgruntlement. A man in his thirties appeared to be the leader as he was the one who brandished the loud-speaker, an amplifier that was clearly a veteran of many such protests, being held together with masking tape and good will. His powerful voice and muscular forearms made quite a spectacle but only to the few tourists curious enough to take photos or video footage. To Dino, and other locals, this was almost an everyday event. Even the line of police who formed a thin barrier between the group and the building looked bored by the goings on. Urged on by the ring-leader, the ragamuffin band of land-workers advanced but only a small distance. It was as if an invisible force field stopped them from moving within striking distance of the police, despite the mob out-numbering the 'boys in dark blue' by four to one. In truth, this was more about making a point and some masculine posturing. There were rarely any physical skirmishes with these types of confrontations and, as always, the hard-done-by band of men disbanded meekly a few minutes later, knowing they could go back home to their wives and girlfriends as warriors in their eyes. Brave men who had stood up to the authorities about unfair taxes, lack of subsidies or whatever the remonstration happened to be about that day.

Dino walked on, not even bothering to expend the energy of a disdainful look on whom he considered being pitiful excuses for men. In his eyes, their transparently fruitless protest was merely an excuse to have half a day off working in the fields. It was an excuse to fuel their egos and get drunk on Limoncello before stumbling home in the early hours to their concerned families who had been waiting by their silent phones for news.

Now, entering the much larger and, rarely for Naples, pedestrainised *piazza plebiscito* (the place of the people), Dino could not resist interacting with the young kids who played football there. Joyfully the small boys ran around obeying a few of the rules of the beautiful game and one from their families – to be home by sunset to avoid a stiff clip around the ear. Intercepting a pass that was never meant for him, Dino weaved expertly around the children who were not even a third his age. The infants chose to ignore the unwelcome new player and stood solemnly, waiting for the man to return their ball. After back heeling the ball into a goal marked with jumpers and school bags, Dino dutifully returned the ball to the nearest boy who took it gratefully, avoiding all eye contact. Smiling, Dino continued on his walk home, wondering what might have been if his own promising career in the sport had not been cut short by a badly broken leg at the age of fifteen.

He left the piazza between the embracing pillared arms of the basilica that encircled half the square, and turned from an open expanse and into the ancient crowded old quarter of Naples. As far as Dino was concerned, all life was here. The sedate, the posh, the tourists, the grandiose, all were left behind as one turned into the high street called *via solitaria*. What remains (and that is a lot in Naples) is concentrated here in a crowded cauldron of smells and sounds. Perversely in Italian the name of this road means 'street of the lonely' but the opposite is so clearly the truth today as the constantly busy but narrow lane serves as a trunk for the many branches of smaller alleyways that cross its length all the way up to the summit of the tall hill it straddles. Each of the narrower thoroughfares crossed at right angles with other streets forming a tight grid of squares filled with jagged rows of buildings of various ages. Many were ancient, their impressive doors or stonework belying their great maturity but others were younger, filling a gap left by another that had been felled through ill repair or as a result of bombing in the war.

It was a dark and foreboding place to the uninitiated, even in the daytime, as the close-knit and crammed buildings blocked out much of any sunlight, washing the colours out of the shop fronts and apartments and bathing everything in a permanent grey light. The overall impression was one of a dark mouth of overlapping haphazard rows of decaying teeth, larger buildings representing the molars, smaller ones the biting incisors. This comparison was strengthened by the construction of the buildings themselves that were solid on the outside but open to the elements in the middle like a tooth that had been hollowed out right down to the roots. And if the buildings were teeth then the residents would be considered by some as bacteria – forever milling around inside and out of the decaying shells with chaotic speed and purpose.

Cars were rarely seen in this crowded district as even tiny two-door vehicles were often too big to squeeze through the twisting streets that could abruptly became narrower still. Any vehicles that ventured this way did not leave the quarter unscathed, evidenced by a rainbow of painted scars on the walls that marked the shoulders of the worst bottlenecks. Smaller mopeds had no such issues, tens of them buzzing along each passageway with only pedestrians to distract them as people always coursed the noisy streets here, especially an endless stream of children who darted in and out of doorways along and across the cobbled streets, never caring to look but somehow always avoiding the throbbing vespas.

Dino turned his back on the frenetic street, rotating his key to open the normal sized door that was set into a much larger huge ancient wooden frame. Once inside, he walked briskly along the short but wide corridor, ignoring the post bearing his name that looked suspiciously like demands for payment. Avoiding the industrial sized paint pot and scaffolding frame he made his way to the staircase and pulled himself up the steps, playfully punching the plastic sheets that hung limply from every floor. His apartment (like all the others in the rented building) was in desperate need of repair and these token gestures were the landlord's attempt to show that the walls and ceiling would all be fixed 'soon'. It fooled no one though as the paint and tools were left collecting dust. No workman had been seen wielding them in months.

Bursting into his apartment, Dino wasted no time in flinging himself onto his lumpy and protesting camp-bed, grinning again as he retrieved from his jeans pocket the crumpled banknotes he had acquired earlier on. He knew he should use the bounty to pay at least some of the bills that were piling up in his pigeon-hole downstairs but his debtors could wait another week or so before persuasion would arrive at his door in the form of a couple of burly henchmen. But then a terrifying thought crossed his mind and Dino's face drained as he realized his identity card was missing. Unless he found it he knew he faced a fine of 50 Euros (which was bad enough) combined with the more significant hassle of hours of bureaucracy to obtain a new one and not being able to prove his identity in the mean time at the frequent spot-checks by the local *cabinieri*. With a sigh he abandoned his plans for a snooze and set out again to re-trace his steps. He felt sure he had misplaced his card on the slopes of Mount Vesuvius during his tumble and he set out again to scour the slopes.

Back at the great volcano, another group of tourists peered over the edge and into the gaping crater. Apart from a few slender columns of steam, all seemed dormant from within the fiery beast.

However, only a few yards away in a small automatic monitoring station, recording needles awoke from a long slumber and began to dance jerkily, scratching a familiar pattern on the paper-covered drum.

Dino stomped angrily through the low-lying dusty green scrub at the base of the volcano, keeping his eyes to the ground to avoid tripping over the larger rocks. Briefly he looked up, just to make sure the tourists he had duped earlier were not scanning the scree for him, still hell-bent on vengeance. He could not see them and he was not surprised. They would have gone back to their plush hotel that was probably in the tacky resort of Sorrento rather than the much closer but less picturesque Naples, not expecting him to return to the scene of the crime. In fact nobody was around right now, it was eerily quiet for this time of day. Normally many groups of colourful holiday-makers could be spotted with their garish shorts and sun burnt legs in the mid-afternoon. (The Americans were always the easiest to spot as they were generally larger than most and you could hear their loud expletives when they were told there was no way to reach the summit without walking.)

Dino quickly forgot the strange absence of tourists as he pressed onwards and upwards looking for his small dark wallet in an area filled with small dark stones. Thankfully after another few minutes searching he saw something that would help him as he stumbled across a darker stripe that stretched ahead of him up the mountain in roughly a straight line. He knew straight away it was the scar he had etched earlier, his heavy tumble pushing loose stones away from their precarious positions, revealing a deeper layer that contained slightly more moisture, darkening the pointed shards of rock. All he had to do now was to carefully scan this metre-wide stretch as he ascended. Somewhere around this line he was sure to find his identity card. Like a naturalist tracking the path of a small insect he walked slowly and thoughtfully with a stooped back, his hands clasped at the base of his spine.

Deep in concentration, Dino did not notice the gentle rumblings that had began beneath his feet and the steam and smoke that was now billowing softly from the aperture of the volcano a few hundred metres above him. He did not know that the reason for the popular volcano being so eerily quiet was due to it being very recently evacuated following an eruption warning. He had not seen the blocked roads and paths as he had retraced his steps through the dense arid forest, normally used only by animals. He was also blissfully unaware that on the opposite slope the eruption had already started – glowing lava being spat furiously high into the air before falling as hot rocks, singeing the ground where each pellet landed. In little time, more magma coalesced beneath the earth and welled into a rising, boiling mass that emerged over the lip of the crater and sluggishly made its way down the mountainside, like a sleepy, venomous snake. Only its high viscosity slowed its advance but it did not lessen its deadly force, the few small bushes that eked out a living on the barren upper slopes cowardly combusting well before they were finally engulfed by the fiery tongue.

Back on the other side of Vesuvius, Dino was becoming increasingly frustrated as he reached the half-way point up the slope. His concentration had not waned though and he barely perceived the strengthening odour of rotten eggs in the air from the sulphur dioxide that was being pumped out in increasing concentrations. At last, he spotted something a little way off the path. Sweating from the excursion in the increasing heat he bounded over. Finally he had found it! Triumphantly he held his identity card aloft and above his dizzying head, the victorious gesture coinciding with a powerful explosion from the crater above him. Frozen by confusion and light-headedness, he watched helplessly as the first of the blazing hot lumps of lava rained down just a few feet from where he stood. It was like a daytime fireworks display, the glowing shapes raining down continuously in a lethal shower of molten pumice. Dino was finally spurred into action when one lump almost grazed his head on its way to the ground. He turned on his heels just as the protrusion of lava that had been making progress on the opposite side rounded the corner to face him. Shocked, he started to make his descent with a little more control than last time but even so his quick run turned into a slide at some points. As he raced he looked over his left shoulder and didn't like what he saw. The lava flow was gaining pace at an unlikely speed and it had now been joined in the race down the mountain side by a second flow! If the volcano could be imagined as a giant headless neck then the two flows of iridescent molten rock

60

were two ends of a scarf that to Dino's horror were racing past him to form a knot beneath him! Fighting against his primeval instincts to flee, he stopped just as the two flows joined a few metres in front of him, the gluey liquid cooling and crumpling as the rivers met. Dino was trapped and felt it was only a matter of time before the thickening flows tightened the knot with his burnt body entwined inside the two strands. He mused that perhaps the better fate now would be to fall unconscious first from the stifling heat and desiccated air that was already burning his throat and stinging his eyes. And yet he had not given up hope yet. Like a trapped animal he spun this way and that, looking for any means of escape, determined not to befall the same fate as the residents of Pompeii nearly two millennia before him but it was hopeless, there was no break in the red hot lava through which to bolt to safety. The area he stood in was now little bigger than a tennis court and shrinking all the time.

Finally he sat down, resigned to his fate as he stared towards Naples and the cool sea beyond that was now seen through a shimmering haze as the scorching hot air all around him distorted the image. He was finding it difficult to breathe now but he knew the end was near as the lava encroached, reducing his island of scree to the size of a squash court.

Dino mused it was such a cliché but it seemed it was true what they say in moments like this – your life really does flash in front of his eyes. It was not like the movies though. The sequence of images did not start with his first memories and his mind's eye was not bordered in a soft focus – everything was crystal clear like a hallucination, probably helped along by the sulphurous fumes and the intensifying heat. The events that played in his mind were snapshots of his life, often just a few seconds of truncated action that then switched without warning to a different moment in time, as if all the key incidents in his life were actors desperately jostling for position at a stage audition. Or, more likely, that he was in an armchair in front of the TV, vacantly flicking through channels that all showed 'made-for-TV' movies based around his life. What surprised Dino was that imbedded in these real recollections were visions of possible futures, none of which he would now ever enact. He watched an older version of himself (slightly more stout and greying at the temples) walking out of a church with a faceless bride on his arm. Then his mind lurched back to his early youth – he was peering up and over the edge of a hospital bed, looking inquisitively at his tired mother, her hair wet from perspiration as she held his new baby brother. Next, he was a bit older, being chased down the street by a portly market seller when he was a young boy, trying to hold onto his stolen bounty of ripe tomatoes as he ran.

The images continued as the unrelenting lava closed in on both sides like a dreary eyelid slowly clamping shut. Dino was now almost unaware of the outside world, how fast he was breathing the hot, poisonous air or how near the deadly red river was to engulfing him. He closed his eyes and felt his feet become warm and then hot as the weight of the scolding lava fell clumsily over them. He could not yet feel pain and wondered if he would be spared that fate as his head became increasingly dizzy from lack of oxygen and heat. Sweat now poured off his brow and onto his shirt but this did nothing to cool him. He felt like he was slowly sinking into a hot bath, even thinking he could hear the water pouring around him. Faster he sank until he hit the bottom of the bath with a thud. At least it was cool here he thought.

Dino awoke. He had no idea how long he had been asleep. At first he was too scared to open his eyes - almost like a patient after an operation afraid that somehow the anaesthetic had worn off too early – but eventually he forced his eyelids open. Was he in hell or perhaps some sort of limbo? His head was pounding, not helped by someone (or something) knocking loudly. Around him cold water flowed. He looked up to find the owner of the rapping knuckles but could only see a devilish ring of fire from which a small orange orb emerged, dropping into the cold water around him with a sizzle. Regaining his faculties, he suddenly understood where he was and what had happened. The weight of the lava around him must have weakened the soil above an old buried roman water channel and into that he had plopped. All he had to do now was follow the water down the underground culvert and to safety. He smiled, knowing he would live to fight another day, perhaps making that dream of marriage to a beautiful woman a reality although he promised himself he would not have a paunch on his big day!

I-IX – VATICANO

The funeral of the Pope came and went without a hitch. The world did not suspect a thing and why would they? He was an old man and it was his time to join God.

The Camerlengo did not believe in God anymore but knew if there really was a heaven he would be going swiftly in the opposite direction when the time came to meet his maker. Still, he had no time for such thoughts. The attention of the world, its people and its assembled media was beginning to move their focus from one side of St. Peter's square to the other. The Pope had barely been laid to rest in the crypt below the ancient church when the cameras of the world's TV stations shifted their attention to the Sistine Chapel. This was where the conclave was about to be held.

Under Michelangelo's masterpiece on the great ceiling, the College of Cardinals solemnly began to file in through the great doors. A few looked up in awe at the famous depictions of heaven and hell but most looked straight ahead – shunning a unique opportunity to gaze at the invaluable artwork without having to battle through the melee of tourists attempting to take strictly forbidden photos or video footage from cameras concealed underneath their garments. Free from the impediment of the absent crowd, the cardinals moved swiftly across the hall, their shadows elongating away from the natural light behind them and mingling with the tortured souls from Hades painted at the base of the great walls.

The task of the cardinals at the conclave was to elect a new Bishop of Rome from amongst their number. That Bishop would then automatically become the new Pope, the head of the Catholic Church and God's conduit on this earth. The holy men hailed from all over the world, the great Catholic church being represented in almost every country on the globe (even if some bishops represented only a few thousand souls where other religions or sects dominated). However, out of the twenty-four bishops in the great room, only half a dozen at most would have a realistic chance of being the next pope as others were too young, too inexperienced or simply not liked enough amongst their peers.

The front-runners for the papal vacancy (according the bookmakers, who were rarely wrong) were as follows –

Cardinal John Schwarz (Aged 59), San Francisco, U.S.A. (Odds – 8/1)

Electing the Californian Cardinal would be seen as a radical, right-wing choice. Fiercely anti-abortion but loved by his flock as a "brash, no-nonsense, larger-than life all-American catholic", he has been praised for his ability for bring Catholicism to the masses with open air services combined with family hog roasts and chilli cook-offs.

Cardinal Bruce Kennedy (Aged 72), Adelaide, Australia (Odds – 6/1)

Bruce could easily be described as an "old-school traditionalist" in a way that only ultra-conservative antipodeans could be. His views (which many would say were 'embarrassingly outdated') are embraced by many in a country that in its thinking often has more in common with austere post-war Britain than its current day Western forbearers. Bruce always delivers his sermons like verbal cannonballs fired down from his lofty pulpit with such fire and brimstone that his salt-and-pepper toupee appears to shake as if it was a skittish furry animal.

Cardinal Estefan Estaba (Aged 75), Caracas, Venezuela (Odds – 4/1 Favourite)

The Cardinal representing South America is the overwhelming favourite and it is not difficult to see why. The heavily moustachioed and bushy eye-browed native American descendant is universally liked by all within the Vatican. The reformed wrestler and unlicensed money lender is ambitious and always tows the 'party line' when it comes to crucial issues such as marriage, attempting to ban condoms and why dinosaurs are not mentioned in the bible. Fluent in seven languages, he is also best placed to be a world-wide mouthpiece for the views of the church when the Latin language proves an impenetrable barrier.

64

The Swiss candidate is little known outside (or indeed inside) Switzerland. Despite his German-sounding name (a legacy of some distant German ancestry on his father's side) Hans-Dieter is staunchly nationalistic. There are even rumours that when he was a youth he was a member of the ultra-left wing "Tut Romansch" (All Romansch) people's party. He cannot be considered a 'serious' prospect for the 'post with the pointed hat' but admittedly he is the only other candidate with enough experience, despite his relatively young age.

As the last of the very reverend clergy, (the almost crippled Bishop Tomasz Bergsson of Sweden), shuffled through the double doors, they were quickly closed and locked behind him by two burly Swiss Guards. The huge ceremonial key was then removed leaving the bishops in seclusion or *cum clave* (literally 'under key' or in modern wording 'under lock') and imprisoned until they chose a new pope.

The assembled high-ranking clergy in their fine flowing robes all took their allocated seats at the simple but ancient wooden benches that had been scratched, etched and pockmarked by countless cabals of bishops over the centuries on numerous occasions exactly like the one that day.

Some took longer than others to find their seats marked with paper place-marks ordained with their names in expert gothic calligraphy. A few were lucky and happened upon their places quickly, others roaming the aisles of tables and benches like lost sheep. The remainder fumbled beneath many layers of expensive clothing in order to produce reading glasses to aid failing sight so they could scan the paper markers. Finally the last (predictably the practically infirm Cardinal George Nascimentala of Western Otogo, New Zealand) carefully placed his bony behind on the uneven bench, only after his very own travelling cushion had been positioned first to ease his aching joints.

All eyes looked now looked forward. The old pope had reined for many, many years so none of the cardinals were present at the last cum clave when the now recently deceased pontiff had been elected. However, all had been briefed well enough to know that once they were all seated, the Camerlengo would appear in front of them at the end of the room and would address them all to remind them of their duties and the process of voting in a new head of the Catholic Church.

Somewhere, a few metres deeper into the secret bowels behind the Sistine Chapel, a door was slammed. The sound was muffled to the ears of the cardinals but it was unmistakable. Old hearts that dared the risk beat faster, others looked upwards towards God, thanking him for the privilege to serve His Holiness in this most reverential of talent contents.

Silently the Camerlengo swept into the chapel from a secret door and stood centrally in front of them all, his arms and open palms flowing outwards and towards the table in front of him. Various objects were placed on that table including neatly cut scraps of parchment the cardinals would use to write the name of their desired candidate; a ballot box in which the votes would be cast and two bowls of powder, (one coloured grey and the other white).

Shortly the bishops would commence their discussions that they hoped would lead to the election of a new pope. If no candidate gained an overall majority from the first ballot the grey powder would be thrown into a bespoke kiln, a chimney carrying the smoke up to the roof of the chapel to be seen by the outside world. The process would be repeated until one candidate had the backing of more than half the room and the white powder would make smoke of the same hue to tell the world that a new pope had been chosen.

The doors to the voting chamber were safely locked and the papal candidates knew they could now relax. The eyes of the world were trained on this building but nobody would gain even an inkling of what would transpire within.

Cardinal Kennedy was the first to break the silence. "Right then, let's get this thing started - who's firing up the barbie?"

"Hallelujah, I hear you brother!" echoed the rotund representative from California. "There had better be some good, fat rib-eyes on the grill," he continued, giving his antipodean rival a 'high five'. The rest of the cardinals all guffawed and began to unwind, some even shedding their dour ceremonial robes to reveal their own comfortable clothing underneath.

The Camerlengo raised a half-hearted smile at the mention of their meal. "I'm afraid that we are only offering traditional Italian food today but I assure you that the quality of the fine cured meats, pizza and pasta is of such high quality it may make your heart skip a beat or two. And of course we will have a plentiful supply of local wines and spirits that your assistants will be bringing out forthwith."

Other members of the church not 'in the know' (and indeed the wider world) would no doubt be shocked and horrified by the events that commonly unfolded during a papal conclave although the very irreverence of the proceedings is almost as old as the ceremony itself. Indeed, as long ago as the 13th century the cardinals were having such a first-rate time during one of the closeted proceedings that they decided they would rather stay happily in seclusion with an endless supply of food and wine, rather than get down to the sobering business of voting for the new pope. After all, it was much more fun than the frugal lifestyle they conducted back in their own countries. On that occasion (following the death of Clement IV in 1268) the church authorities to take drastic actions to urge a vote, removing the roof so that the cardinals were open to the elements. When even that failed, their food (and more importantly their wine) was then severely rationed. Lo and behold a new pope was elected within a matter of hours and the party was over.

Over the proceeding decades and centuries, the cardinals began to behave themselves more in the papal conclaves. However, a vestige of those less than holy practices still carries on to this day and cardinals know that a day or two of drunken revelry can be expected before the serious discussions of voting in a new pope can begin…once the hangovers have subsided of course.

Presently the food was brought out to the clergy, the fare simply displayed on silver plates. The candidates salivated visibly as they spied the edible treats. It was no surprise the old men were drooling as the catering at the papal conclaves was legendary, only the best produce being used from the newly deceased Pope's personal pantry. Traditionally, the conclaves were used to make the most of the now unwanted fresh goods that would not be ingested by the decomposing pontiff so it did not go to waste – a kind of Shrove

Tuesday if you will. Today, the ingredients were bought in for the occasion with a flagrant disregard to costs.

As the last of the diminutive servants tried not to buckle under the weight of a huge tray supporting a pizza the size of a wagon wheel, the first of the servants had returned with a large carafe of wine, the contents sloshing over the rim as the serf lost his footing on the uneven medieval flag-stone floor.

The high jinks and the fervent banging of utensils was momentarily suspended as the bishops sated their churning empty stomachs by noisily tucking in to slices of pizza. Manners were forgotten as everyone greedily tore a floppy wedge from the huge circular dishes, the scene resembling a pride of emaciated lions dismembering a befallen wildebeest. Within a few short minutes only a handful of breadcrumbs and a lingering smell of mixed herbs remained as meagre evidence that food had been lain out before them. Satisfied, the clergy all relaxed in their own ways. Some chatted in small groups conversing about the latest ecclesiastical issues whereas others preferred to be alone in their own company, deep in thought or thumbing through the manifestoes produced by the papal candidates.

Suddenly the mood in the room changed. The frailest and most elderly cardinal (Nascimentala from New Zealand) was bent double emitting a devilish growl from deep within himself, his left arm shaking like a twig in a gale as he tried to keep himself upright. He failed and within moments he collapsed in a motionless heap on the floor. The other cardinals were stunned but before they had time to break free from their temporary petrifaction and help their stricken colleague, another of their number became unwell. The overweight Cardinal Schwarz from California (until now one of the favourites for the ultimate prize) clutched his chest and keeled over dramatically.

The Camerlengo stood impassively as he watched the proceedings, not even moving a muscle as the other cardinals plaintively hobbled towards him, a hellish pastiche of plaintive and frightened faces. The Camerlengo failed to respond and, one by one, the papal candidates dropped to the floor like so many sacks of potatoes. As the last outstretched arm made it to within an inch of the Camerlengo's highly polished left boot he was already moving away to the back of the room to prepare the white powder to throw onto the fire. All the cardinals were scattered around the room, dead or in the final throws of their own fatality. All that is except one – the mysterious Cardinal Vilhelm from Switzerland who had remained calm in his seat the whole time, seemingly reading the manifestoes of the other candidates.

The only two men who were going to come out of that room alive slowly made their way to each other, looking down to make sure of their footing on the uneven carpet of corpses.

"Congratulations Hans-Dieter," the Camerlengo said, firmly shaking the hand of the older man. "I guess as you are the only remaining candidate, you must, by default, be the new Pope!"

"Why thank you Camerlengo," the cardinal responded. "Long live Switzerland and the latest extension to its territories…The Vatican City!". At this both men cackled in a most evil manner and calmly made their way to the front of the room where the special bowls of powder lay. Coldly they enacted what they had rehearsed in their heads many times since this bizarre proposal was put to them. Such a simple act of throwing a brilliant white powder onto the open fire that would have such complex consequences once the smoke it produced reached the roof.

And so the signal was sent by the ancient method. A message delivered from this most private of rooms directly up the chimney and out into the most public of arenas where they knew the eyes of the world were watching. The two men could not possibly hear the reaction of the throng, bated by fervent anticipation, but they knew any cheers would turn to a blessed stunned silence in a few short minutes.

The Camerlengo's two bumbling assistants were characteristically dozing when a great earth-shaking roar stirred them from their slumber like a pair of hibernating bears being awoken early from their winter sleep by a low-flying jet engine. Immediately they stood to attention, pre-conditioned to respond to loud stimuli in this manner as it usually meant the Camerlengo had caught them sleeping on the job again and had slammed a door in frustration. Their master was not here but this particular noise meant they could not go back to sleep. Sighing in unison, they trudged through from the ante room to the Sistine chapel and grabbed the first of the dead cardinals, each rushing to what they assumed would be the lightest corpse, neither wishing to overburden their wide but sloping shoulders.

Outside the sturdy external walls of the Sistine Chapel, the mood of the jubilant crowd gave way from excitable pregnant anticipation to one of sheer bedlam at the sight of the white smoke snaking out of the ancient chimney. Television reporters (whose vans encircled the giant square) scurried into position in front of their transmitting cameras, ensuring the chapel in the background over their left shoulders. Networks from around the globe finished their exhaustive build-up and prepared to go 'live' to the scene for the great announcement. Everyone looked up and waited for the tell-tale twitch of the red curtain which meant the new Pope was about to emerge after being fitted with the papal tunic. (Incidentally, the simple tunic came in three sizes to fit all popes, whatever their height or girth).

Lucinda Lammergeyer, the resident 'overseas' correspondent for the American YUC television news corporation, took a final hurried look at the state of her oily T-zone in her tiny compact mirror before the short countdown began. Within ten seconds she would be reporting live in front of literally hundreds or maybe even thousands of avid viewers back home. This was her big break after the unfortunate death of her supervisor and 'overseas' news anchor Brad Bradowski and she was determined not to screw it up. "Good afternoon Youngstown, Ohio!" the young woman warbled annoyingly, trying to 'engage' with the camera. "I am standing at the epicentre of old world events here today as we await the arrival of the newly crowned Pope."

The poor choice of the word 'crowned' instead of 'elected' would be lost on most, if not all of the largely disinterested viewers who were absently watching proceedings. Also lost on the coach potatoes (and practically everyone else) was a luxury coach edging its way out of the back of the square. The coach (fitted with bomb-proof glass and re-enforced with layers of Kevlar) ferried the unsuccessful papal candidates out of the Vatican. This was normal practice, no candidate wished to hang around after the other guy had got the job, except that normally the cardinals would all be alive.

At the business end of the square, Lucinda Lammergeyer squawked into the camera as she awaited the papal appearance, her verbiage dripping with unwanted and over-exorbitant explanation like a verbal Christmas tree bowing under the weight of garish lights, tinsel and other flashing adornments. Her excitement was palpable and unbearable but certainly not adorable as she had hoped. Her personal excitement as a good catholic girl being able to witness something like this first hand was to the detriment of her delivery and future job prospects. Mercifully, for all the viewers of Youngstown, Ohio, she was reverentially quiet as the new pope Cardinal Wilhelm confidently swept the red curtain aside and stepped onto the balcony. Many were surprised when they saw who had succeeded. It was not one of the front runners for the position but then most commentators and experts agreed that occasionally an outsider was victorious as the wishes of the few cardinals who voted where never known, only supposed. (If only the world knew that actually no one had voted and all the other candidates had been murdered by means of poison, their bloated corpses heading towards a roundabout in central Rome at increasing velocity on a coach packed with various explosive devices.)

Not many people then saw the Swiss Guards spilling out from hidden orifices behind the pillars that ringed St. Mark's square and even less realized this was not part of the proceedings. However, everyone heard the explosion and saw the mushrooming orange and grey plume rising up from behind a row of buildings a few hundred yards away. Everyone also watched on as the Swiss Guards produced automatic weapons from beneath their tunics, the nozzles pointing inwards from their ring of force towards the crowd like a Venus-fly trap that had been triggered to bring in its stiff hair-like protrusions, ensnaring its pray.

71

I-X – MILANO

The caretaker fumbled badly as he tried to force the key into the lock, shaking with the rigours of old age as the metal probe finally found its home. Wincing with the strain on his arthritic wrist he turned the heavy mechanism. The handle released with a clank, the air rushing out to greet the face of the caretaker, seemingly grateful to escape the near air-tight conditions it had been housed in overnight. The air was normally fetid at best, the old damp building not ventilated properly to dissipate the odours of sweaty tourists from the previous day but this morning the foul air was enriched with the acrid smell of burnt plastic. The caretaker scowled, expecting to see a dozing security guard fast asleep next to a melted plastic plate pilfered from the canteen and used a makeshift ashtray, the flammable dish catching light when the abandoned cancer stick had ignited the flammable material. (How the obese thug slept through the toxic fumes was beyond him he thought but maybe those horrible cheap paper tubes filled with factory scrapings had ruined his sense of smell many years before.)

He hobbled over to the large bank of light switches on the opposite wall, a torch lighting his way as it was still dark in this dank basement room with no windows to provide any natural light. Methodically he flicked each switch in turn, subconsciously registering the series of sharp 'clicks' as each neon filled light glowed reluctantly into life. The last switch flicked, he instinctively turned to face the security guard but the rotund watchman was nowhere to be seen, his simple chair neatly stowed against the small table he used to lean on to read his comics alone through his nocturnal vigil.

Shaking his head with disdain at the security guard slinking off early, he turned towards the large object that nearly filled the room. The smell of burnt plastic forgotten, he dutifully checked off the few points on his visual inspection list, eager to return upstairs as soon as possible, back to the light and the cleaner air of his little office and away from the stale and enclosed room that for some reason always sent shivers down his spine.

1. *Overhead lights working? CHECK.*
2. *Model lights working? CHECK.*
3. *Model ready for visitors? CH….*

The caretaker stopped and stared intently at the model. Normally he barely even gave it a second look. After all, it was an intricate thing and he was a mere caretaker, how on earth was he meant to spot if some tiny thing was out of place? He did not get paid enough for a detailed look at every tree and building to see if it had somehow fallen on a piece of train track. Today was very different though, even he could see that something was wrong. Very wrong.

Quickly he stepped over for a closer look, an ironic smile growing across his face. The security guard had really done it this time. He had been warned about smoking in the model room before but he never listened. This would get him the sack for sure. What a mess! He saw to his amusement that the oaf had not just melted part of the model with a carelessly discarded cigarette but had also started destroying parts of the scale model itself! No wonder the idiot had sidled off early rather than stay to explain this disarray. The caretaker wondered what on earth the guard had been thinking, or whether he had just been drunk on cheap grappa. The caretaker proceeded to gleefully note down every detail of the damage to relay to the managers when they arrived.

Stretched out in front of the decrepit but diligent caretaker was the largest model railway in the world. In this room the major and minor railway lines for the whole of Italy were depicted in their exact positions at a scale of 1:500 from the alps in the north to the Mediterranean sea in the south, the twisting tracks carving through tunnels burrowed into polystyrene hills and snaking around lakes of hard resin.

This was the realisation of a boyhood dream of a man who became obsessed with model railways at a very early age. Luckily for him he was born into almost immeasurable wealth and upon reaching adulthood he was easily able to find the funds and the workforce required to achieve his vision. Even so, during its lengthy construction he had been called 'eccentric' at best and simply 'mad' by most. However, most people ate their words when the marvel finally opened its doors to the public after five years of planning and nearly the same time required for its intricate construction. When in full flow, over one hundred trains simultaneously streaked along the tracks, racing along at break-neck scaled speeds. Even so, the model was so vast that travelling the model distance from Rome to Venice still took a few minutes in real time.

The train engines were all controlled by a bespoke computer programme that whirled away in a small room out of sight. Tens of staff were on hand around the great table to leap into action for the rare event of a train breaking down or coming off the tracks, a network of cleverly concealed holes and trap-doors in the polystyrene hills and mountains providing the maintenance access. The paying public, who arrived daily in their droves, were able to walk around the model at a discrete distance (just far enough to ensure no outstretched hands could touch the replica) or view from a series of platforms and walkways suspended above the immense arrangement. People were always in awe at the miniature world, many staying for a couple of hours to witness day turn to night and back again as time raced by at twelve model hours to one in real time.

The caretaker finished up and thankfully left the dark room that would see no visitors for days. The whole place would have to be shut until the damage could be repaired by especially hired artisans, costing the company hundreds of thousands. The security guard would surely pay for his carelessness (or was it wanton destruction?) with his job and a criminal prosecution would no doubt follow with evidence from the surveillance tapes that would have been recording all night.

The caretaker never got to see the tapes as they were snatched by the management before he got the chance but he would have undoubtedly been astonished at what they showed. They proved that nobody entered the room at all that night, the security guard having been given the night off by the owner himself, or so the absent guard later claimed. Therefore the cause of the damage could not be laid at

his great fat feet, the video clearly showing the damage was caused
suddenly and inexplicably.

Caretaker's notes – 6.43am, Saturday 27th March.

Locks: All secure
Alarm: On
Video: On
Lights: Off on arrival
Model Condition: Major damage to some sections

Notes:
The model has been vandalized in several places, apparently by
different methods. There is no sign of forced entry and the alarms are
all working so I can only conclude that the security guard was to
blame.

Details of damage –

Section: VENEZIA (VE_002, VE_197)
Damage: The resin 'water' has been melted in places,
'flooding' the city. Gondolier figure embedded in lagoon.
Cause: Cigarette?

Section: ROMA (RO_012)
Damage: Minor. Model car and section of wall damaged.
Cause: Drunk security guard playing with car?

Section: BOLOGNA (BO_042, BO_014)
Damage: Many buildings partially or wholly destroyed. Small
pebbles in the streets and some model figures moved.
Cause: Pebbles from beach in Rimini section moved by
security guard and rolled like marbles?

Section: NAPOLI (NA_055)

Damage: Solder covering side of volcano. Model trees, part of
volcano melted.
Cause: Electrical fault causing solder to melt?

I-XI – VATICANO

The Camerlengo forced the mischievous smile from his face as he opened the doors outwards to the balcony having just delivered the news to the new Pope that the other unsuccessful papal candidates were safely on the journey home…to heaven!

Thousands had waved the coach out of the Vatican and saw it turn onto the Ponte Sant'Angelo that crossed the Tiber river into Rome. Thousands more then looked on aghast as it swerved into the barriers, bursting into flames before plunging into the river. Witnesses recounted there would be no survivors but of course, unbeknownst to all, the occupants were already dead anyway.

Stepping back, the Camerlengo allowed the new Pope to shuffle forward in his traditional velvet slippers and out into the bright sunlight. The head of the Roman Catholic church waved his arms gently to the crowds in a humble manner. The new pope felt far from humble though, quite the opposite in fact, wondering if Hitler had felt this way when he had addressed his own adoring masses at the famous rallies in the years preceding the Second World War. The noise was deafening as the occupants of the packed St. Marks square ululated as one towards the balcony. The pope stepped forward slowly towards the podium, each step seemingly having a calming effect on the mix of clergy, church-goers, media and interested others below him. As the new pontiff clasped each side of the modern transparent lectern, gigantic Vatican flags unfurled themselves around the circular enclosure, the serene mustard and white colours adding to the splendour of the occasion.

Immediately the crowd silenced itself as the immense congregation prepared itself to witness the first public address of the new Bishop of Rome. The excitement was understandable. In these tough times, everyone of a catholic faith (and many others besides) were eager to hear the essence of what direction he intended to take the church during his time in the highest office. Of course, the majority of those watching would not understand the speech delivered in Italian but many had earpieces tuned into radio stations that would attempt an almost instant translation. Others were happy just to be there at this most rare of occasions and hear his voice in person.

The Pope began to speak, the vast majority of observers not noticing any difference to the types of sermon delivered hundreds of times before by other Popes over the preceding decades and centuries. It was soon apparent to most though that the Pope was not speaking in Italian. The words appeared familiar to those who spoke Italian and Spanish, even though it seemed the odd unknown word from another dialect had crept in to the passage. Perhaps the Pope was adding a few words from his own German lexicon some pondered? Highly unusual but maybe he wished to start a new trend of the pontiff speaking partly in his own mother tongue? The manner did seem more fervent though – most had to admit that.

After a quiet start, the Pope was no longer reading calmly from his notes but staring out wildly into the square, even pointing and thumping his closed fists on the plastic lectern in front of him. The watching public thought this new Pope was full of fire and brimstone, that was for sure. Those that had opted for a radio translation had given up half way through as for some reason all broadcasts had ceased with no explanation provided. They removed their earphones and continued to watch and listen in adoration without understanding, like a toddler watching their parents talk between each other when words were just a cascade of incomprehensible sounds.

Only a small handful within the square understood the full meaning of what was happening. Some ran from the square in fear, followed by perplexed looks. Others stood with mouths wide open, the colour draining from their faces in utter disbelief. If it was not the Pope himself speaking these words they would have said it had to be a cruel hoax.

In the outside world, the media and authorities were catching on more quickly than the assembled masses in the square. When television and radio stations realized that the Pope was not speaking Italian, automatic translation programs were used to analyze the strange tongue. Within seconds they determined the dialect and deciphered the meaning. Breaking news tickers popped up on news channels with the translated highlights, interrupting normal programming as the relevant authorities were informed. The story of the decade had just turned into the story of the century.

With a final flourish The Pope ended his dictum at the top of his voice screaming *"In per tuts, tuts per in!"* Stepping back from the podium he flung his arms wide to the adoring people who were still almost to man blissfully unaware of what this rousing speech entailed. All around the perimeter of the great square, new flags were being unfurled from the roofs of the great Vatican buildings, neatly covering the yellow and white of the Vatican. These, however, were red with a white cross. It was the flag of Switzerland that was now being proudly displayed, the famous emblem now also emblazoned on the chest on the Pope who had ripped open his papal tunic to reveal his own garments hewn from the same bold design.

The reason why so few had understood his speech was because it had been delivered in *Romansch*, the true language of the people of Switzerland, a speech that ended with the motto of that fiercely independent country, one that translated into English as *"One for all, all for one!"*.

II

THE SENTINAL NEWPAPER, London, Tuesday 4ᵗʰ August

SWISS ARMY OCCUPIES VATICAN CITY WITH FORCE

Confusion reigns in the centre of Rome as, for the first time in almost a millennia, the Vatican City has been invaded by forces from another country.

In a strange twist, one of many since the outgoing pope Vincenzo Bassi passed away last week, the invading forces came from within in the form of the formally staunchly loyal Swiss Guards who were thought to be a largely ceremonial and impotent force. However, their clear militarian stance at the unveiling of the new Pope yesterday suggested more malevolent tendencies that were reinforced when they branded their rifles as the Swiss national flag was unveiled around St. Peters Square in front of shocked tourists and officials alike.

The new incumbent Pope, a virtually unknown Swiss national, appeared to be an integral part of the plot, addressing the congregation in Swiss dialect instead of the traditional Latin that….

…the leader of the coalition Swiss government was quick to distance himself, his government and the regular Swiss army from the unbelievable actions taken by the guards yesterday, describing events as being like "something out of a fiction novel". He went on to say…

…an immediate and hastily arranged meeting of the UN, the Italian Government and various heads of state from the EU confided secretly that there were currently "no options available" to deal with this "unprecedented scenario" of how to remove the new pope (and the Swiss guards that now protected him with force) without "breaking every international law in the book".

SWISS ROLL IN! POPE HOPE? NOPE!

The world was STUNNED on Monday when new Pope Hans-Deiter Wilhelm, 44, took office and straight away claimed The Vatican City in the name of his home country of SWITZERLAND!

The Swiss Guards, (who wear colourful pyjamas) gave a show of force, pointing their semi-automatic weapons at the crowd and advancing at on-lookers once the Pope had finished his speech. At the time of writing the personal army of some 500 strong men were parading the perimeter of the Vatican, stopping anyone coming or going through the small state's four entrances.

Rae Gorman, 23, has lived and worked in Rome for four years as a "barmaid" and saw the events unfold first hand. "I couldn't believe it!" she exclusively told our reporter, "You expect better of someone so religious!".

The Swiss government has denied any involvement, saying the coup must have been masterminded by an eccentric billionaire or a terrorist cell.

EDITORIAL COMMENT - We here at "The Sky" do not believe the cocky moustachioed Alp-dwellers and urge all of our readers to boycott all Swiss goods and services until they admit responsibility and withdraw from The Vatican so that new and fair Pope elections can be held.

For a full list of Swiss products and services to boycott, please visit our website but here are few obvious starters – Banks, Cheese(with holes in), watches, chocolate, Nestle products, cuckoo clocks, Roger Federer.

II-I – A PILGRIMAGE

Four young people were unaware of the new turmoil unfolding in the very heart of Rome as they made their way towards the eye of this great storm. Each travelled in search of a new life, unaware of their true purpose and that the hopes of millions would rest on their shoulders within the next few hours.

Despite the quartet all arriving from different cities, leaving at varying times, they all unknowingly disembarked within a few minutes of each other at the sprawling Termini railway station in the centre of the city. They were all running late and not wishing to be tardy for their appointment, a time that was stressed as being non-negotiable, they all separately rushed towards what they thought would be the quickest mode of transport for the final leg of their journey.

Laura and Dino both headed for the taxi rank outside the station, ignoring the beggars and drunks that ambled outside in the adjoining courtyard and bus terminal like sluggish creatures made of cloth rags. Across the road from the taxi rank, shop proprietors hawked business outside their shabby but colourful one-story shops, lackadaisically waving mobile phone covers, sunglasses and even cheap umbrellas in the paths of mildly agitated commuters and precocious youths in the hope of a quick sale. It was Laura who was the first to successfully attract the attention of a passing taxi, the driver, like most men, not being able to resist her plaintive form. As the car skid to a halt she barked out her destination through the now open window. This part of the ritual was merely a formality as the sweaty driver had already decided he would be happy to take her wherever she wanted to go, even reaching behind him to open the rear passenger door for her.

It was not Laura though who took advantage of the open door but Dino who had snuck up on the dirty cab with stealth, almost diving in through the gap and onto the back seat as he instructed the driver to leave immediately with a curt *'andiamo'*, *'we go'*. The surprised taxi driver was used to such brash behaviour but was disappointed that his new fare was a lot less pleasing on the eye. Laura, brought up in a more gentile and respectful environment, was less than accepting of his attempt to commandeer her ride. 'Hey! Get out of my cab you filthy urchin," she said with obvious disgust, "This cab was mine!".

"Were you inside the car? Was it driving off? I don't think so lady. It was the last available taxi – I saw it and so I claimed it in the name of the great Dino Capelli," he shouted defiantly, sitting upright and securing the seatbelt across his lap, not to protect himself from any possible impact but to help prevent his from removal from the cab.

Laura sighed. She did not want to admit defeat but she knew that here possession was sadly nine tenths of the law. She decided to offer a compromise. "So. Where are you going the *great* Dino Capelli, taxi-stealer extraordinaire?" she asked with a snooty jerk of her head.

Dino smiled back cheekily. "Normally it would be wherever you are going my beautiful but today sadly I cannot as I have pressing and very important business at The Vatican".

"In that case you are lucky as that is also my destination today Capelli. However, seeing as it is *your* taxi ride it only seems right that *you* pay the whole fare!" Her pride just about intact, she tried to ignore the two pairs of eyes watching her negotiate the entry into the car without exposing her upper thighs (and possibly more) as the slit in her skirt rode up – only better men deserved that honour she thought sternly. Once safely inside, she sat cross-legged and pressed herself against the passenger door, as far away as possible from her unwanted, greasy and dirty looking companion.

The show over, the driver pulled away, pleased that the lady was safely aboard. Spending the journey by looking at her through the rear-view mirror would be the highlight of his day and he could tell from her smart dress that she would probably have the means to pay the fare if, as he suspected, the other occupant was unable to produce any coins from his grubby pockets.

Dino was also contented to have some eye-candy to look at although he felt confident that at some point later he would be able to feast with more than just his eyes and would have her phone number in his little black book by the time they parted.

Unconsciously checking her makeup in a pocket mirror produced from her tiny clutch bag, Laura hoped the journey would be short so she could rid herself of these tiresome men. In the mean time she also wished for "Disgusting Dino" to leave her in peace and not try to talk to her as they crept through the Rome traffic. Sadly for her she was to be proven wrong on both counts.

Just a few metres directly beneath that very taxi, Luca was using the underground metro despite having mixed feelings about using that particular mode of transport. Here in Rome this Venetian truly was a fish out of water – uncomfortable enough with the traffic and busy roads above to want to avoid them but still feeling a sense of unease at being underground, something that was practically impossible in Venice as it probably meant you would be drowning. Reluctantly he had decided the underground metro was slightly the lesser of two evils.

Deeper and deeper underground he descended, using stairs and escalators to make progress through the ever narrowing but gracefully curving brick-lined caverns, trying to shake off the uneasy sensation of the increasing volumes of earth, concrete and steel that lay above him. At last he arrived at the correct platform, surprised that the multi-coloured board above his head told him exactly when the next train would be approaching. (This was all very different to Venice where the river buses, the *vaporetti*, seemingly turned up on a whim, whenever *they* decided the time was right instead of adhering to the imposed timetable.) Luca was more shocked when the carriage arrived as it was covered from the top of its roof to the bottom of its wheels in psychedelic graffiti, like a tattoo artist's willing muse. (Graffiti existed in Venice of course but it was always scrubbed off within hours for fear of spoiling the background of the rich tourist's photos, thus threatening their return trip and sullying their holiday recollections to friends and visitors who then may be deterred from visiting at all.)

For a moment he wondered how the budding street artists would have the opportunity to create their artworks. He imagined them poised with a can, finger on the trigger as if it was a pistol, waiting for the few seconds it was in the station to add to their creations whilst avoiding commuters and security guards alike but of course he scolded himself shortly afterwards for his naivety. The kids with spray cans would paint the carriages above ground and in the isolation of night when they were parked in sidings and sheds. The time would allow their works of art to be completed in one sitting although Luca guessed they would never know when or where their grand unveiling would occur on an unsuspecting (and usually uncaring) public at an underground station some miles away the next morning.

Crowds rudely pushed past Luca but this spurred him into action, caught up in a wave of people eager to cram on the carriage in front of him before the doors closed again. Safely on board he found his face almost pressed up against a male armpit, the attached limb held high for an over-head hold, Luca longed for the canals of his home city and the open air that flowed over his gondola. Thankfully the doors were finally closing which did not mean he would be any more comfortable but at least the journey was about to start and therefore logically he was nearer to its end.

The doors were already half shut when an animated figure hurtled into view from around the corner that led to the escalators. Luca was the only one who looked at the young woman as she ran, everyone else already ensconced in their invisible personal cocoons favoured by underground users the world over. Her eyes met with his and his alone, eyes that even from a distance were easily discernible as two striking blue pools. '*Prego!*' she shouted, pleading directly for him to keep the door open for her and without a further thought Luca reached forward to try to stop the doors from closing and, sensing his hands, they sprung open once more. Gratefully Alice leaped aboard, thanking him with a simple word and a captivating, almost child-like smile of innocence as others quietly snarled in their direction, annoyed at this slightest of delays to their commute.

Struck dumb by their whirlwind meeting, Luca could not think of anything to say and slunk back to where he had stood before, behind the armpit. Shyness and intervening heads stopped Luca from attempting to look in Laura's direction again until he sought her azure eyes as he disembarked a few stops later. He was surprised that his heart was beating faster as he looked for her when he left the train and even more astonished when she appeared from nowhere at his side and initiated a conversation as they made their way back to the surface. After every step he felt more comfortable, not knowing if he was relaxing in the company of the young woman or whether he was merely happy to be returning to above ground.

II-II – MILANO

The prisoner thumped the plastic table in his kitchen as he watched the Television set through the window of the adjoining security guard's room. It was clear from the news bulletin he watched that his attempt at control of the outside world had worked to a certain extent but he had failed to stop the emissaries from leaving for Rome. They would probably all be at The Vatican within a matter of hours. He knew the chance of them succeeding was small but he had to eliminate all possibilities until only one remained.

Therefore today was the day he would have to escape and join his ally in The Vatican, where together they would seal their deal and the fate of many others.

II-III – VATICANO

As two young adults skipped out of the exit of Cipro metro station they almost collided with another youthful couple exiting a taxi with equal haste. Exchanging automatic apologies, they moved on in their pairings, unaware they were soon to be united in the same cause.

The first thing all of them saw as they walked towards their final destination was the towering grey walls of the Vatican museum, almost filling their fields of vision. It was a very familiar sight known to all Italians and millions of people around the world but today at the base of the wall they realized there was one key difference to the norm and the first sign that this would not be an average day.

At any time during daylight hours, a long queue of people would normally be waiting patiently to gain entry to the Vatican museums, the line snaking back from the small entrance and up the hill along the city walls. But today that colourful procession had been replaced by a line of Swiss Guards that remained motionless unless a confused tourist wandered up to them to make an enquiry or to take a photo. Any such inquisitor was soon sent back after a curt exchange. Across the road from this show of force, where cheap restaurants and tacky souvenir shops usually squeezed the tourist euro for all it was worth, the normal hustle and bustle of sightseers and pilgrims was replaced by a jostling throng of journalists, reporters and TV vans, all there waiting for a break in the biggest story in decades.

Laura, for one, was not fazed by this unexpected sight as she assumed the paparazzi attention and the parade of Swiss Guards was solely for her arrival. She treated the short walk between her already departed taxi and the door to the museum as her own personal red carpet, gracefully slinking across the road that now appeared to be an agreed no-man's-land between the guards and the media and tourists. She smiled at the photographers who shuffled as near as they dared, snapping away with their expensive cameras just in case *she* was part of the story. When she reached the cordon of army men she proffered her invitation as per the written instructions. A guard scanned the small piece of card and looked at Laura before disappearing inside. Laura smiled politely at the other guards by the door but they did not return the gesture. She was embarrassed at having to wait to gain entry to a place of importance but credentials had to be checked no doubt. Shortly the tip tap sound of steel toed shoes preceded the guard who returned, nodded without emotion and returned the card before standing aside to let her pass through the door behind him.

This caused pandemonium amongst the journalists. Someone had been let into the Vatican for the first time in over 24 hours and with seemingly little fuss! As one they rushed forward, some questioning with microphones held out in front of them, others trying to barge their way through the entrance that was now covered once more with several lines of the pantaloon-wearing guards. The fervour continued until a quick burst of gunfire directed high in the sky soon saw the hacks retreat again to a respectful distance.

Witnessing Laura's successful entry her taxi companion, the ever confident Dino was next to cross the divide between reporters and guards. Holding his invitation card out in front of him like a white handkerchief he pushed his way through the forest of cameras, microphones and man bags with difficulty. Straightening his hair and unbuttoning his shirt to expose what he considered his manly chest, he sauntered across the open tarmac, obviously playing up for the TV cameras that he assumed must have been recording every moment for the crowds watching at home. Like Laura before him, he passed through the lines of armed forces and through the door at their rear after they carefully scrutinized his own credentials. This prompted more consternation from the journalists but the protestations were more subdued than last time, like a footballer on a yellow card berating the referee with caution, not wanting to have a red card brandished above his head, sending him from the field of play.

Almost unnoticed at the rear of the colourful mob of reporters, Luca and Alice looked at each other before they themselves forced their way through and into the open. Together they crossed the void in slight bewilderment and trepidation of the unwanted attention before they reached the soldiers who acted exactly as before. The reaction from the journalists was now barely more than a disgruntled muttering as they snapped away, wishing *they* had these special invitations, whatever they were. At this point, some hacks decided the show was over and packed up, opting to try to penetrate another part of the Vatican's 3,000 metre border in search of that exclusive scoop. Like rats smelling the grain inside a locked barn they could all smell the story fermenting within that ancient fortress.

The four young adults were now suddenly inside The Vatican, across a now patrolled border and technically into another country. However, as they looked around they realized it was not the start to the adventure they had expected. They were alone, the quiet of the sparse surroundings taking a moment to get used to after the din outside. After a few seconds they remembered their manners and introduced themselves to each other with a flurry of kisses, handshakes and quick introductions.

An awkward pause followed before Alice became the first to speak again, her excitement and curiosity finally prompting her as she took in her surroundings. "So, do you think there are cameras in here recording us now or is this just a waiting room before everything starts?"

Dino responded after he took advantage of Alice's gaze being averted to asses her looks. "I can't imagine they would be filming us in here already," he said, coolly crossing his legs as he sat on a cheap old chair with a dodgy leg, "It looks like a forgotten storeroom!"

"Ah, but could this be part of a test?" Luca said quietly, already worrying how he came across on the television, how many people were watching, what his parents would think and wondering if he would regret accepting this strange invitation.

"A test in here? Like what?" Dino replied. "How to escape from a looked room with no windows, no doors apart from the one we came through?!"

"It's possible" responded Luca defensively. "After all, we don't know what is to be expected of us based on these invitations," he said, waving his own card dismissively.

"All I am wondering is whether we can smoke in here," said Laura, fishing around in her bag for a packet of cigarettes, the stress belying her need for nicotine (or something stronger).

"Well seeing as we may all have a little bit of time to ourselves in this little room," Dino responded to nobody in particular, "We may as well all find out our intentions for being here! Starting with myself of course – I guess the reason I accepted the invitation was obvious – the time has come for my numerous talents to be showcased to the nation and indeed the world stage. Somebody in the Vatican hierarchy here has obviously heard about me and hence my pre-approved, "no audition required" invitation to appear on this show flew through my letterbox. All that remains to be seen is what field of fame I will be thrust into at the end of this – my shrewd entrepreneurial skills or my undoubted footballing talent perhaps? I was once cruelly doubted by an inept scout from Napoli but never again!" Finishing his clearly rehearsed (but largely ignored) diatribe, he turned to Alice. "Alyssa, what was *your* reason for accepting?"

"Its *Alice*," she replied, her early excitement replaced by anger at his careless error and unease at the strange surroundings they now found themselves in. With a slightly melancholic tone she continued. "I guess it's similar to you. I am not getting any younger, practically too old to be a dancer in fact, but I want to give the little girl inside me one last chance to achieve the dream life she always wanted. After all, I don't want to have to work in a bar my whole life. So, that is why I accepted as the invitation stated our *"talents would be showcased to the widest possible audience"* whilst we were inside the Vatican so I felt I had to accept."

Without waiting to be prompted, Laura stated her reasons for her attendance. "My motive is quite different from you two. I do not seek fame…although a fortune would be nice," she added absently as she quietly exclaimed some joy at finally finding a cigarette in her bag and immediately began hunting in the bottomless depths once more for a lighter or even a box of matches. "No, my real reason is actually revenge on my boyfriend…sorry *ex*-boyfriend". She paused again as with some relief she found a colourful throwaway lighter. "He went on one of these types of shows last month. I was proud of him at

92

first but he ended up cheating on me with some common German slut...live on air!"

"So, you want to get your own back by having a liaison with someone in here?" Dino said only half in jest with what he hoped was a cheeky smile.

"No thank you. I am off men for the time being. But there are certain facts he may not wanted aired in public. Mind you, if through this process I attract a suitable eligible bachelor then I guess I could be swayed again depending on the size of what he packs in his trousers," Laura replied, teasingly looking at Dino as she provocatively blew smoke in his direction.

Dino smoothed his eyebrows as his smile widened.

"I am referring to his wallet of course before you get any other ideas. And I'm afraid I only go for men of a certain height," she continued, stealing the smile from the face of her overly keen suitor and placing it on her own.

As they all smirked at the put down, the group was startled by a small dull clicking sound that appeared to originate from behind an opposing wall. Transfixed and a little apprehensive, they watched and gasped as part of the wall swung out like a door towards them, revealing darkness behind. They stared, concerned but excited. From the black hidden depths of what lay beyond, something or someone stirred. Dry ice flowed sluggishly out from the doorway, the smoke-like substance disappearing as it dissipated in the warmer air of the room. Music began to play. A poor quality recording of the 'Rocky' theme tune drifted in with the smoke. Who would be coming through the black doorway they wondered? Would it be the host of the show they were all invited to be on? Perhaps even Sylvester Stallone?! Sadly they were all disappointed as a sullen looking man in formal clerical attire finally emerged.

Opening his arms wide he greeted his small congregation. "Welcome to The Vatican my young sheep and my sincere apologies for the theatrics. I told my assistants I wanted to 'make an entrance' and I'm afraid they took my meaning rather literally." He swivelled his head to look behind him, narrowing his eyes at his two small hunchbacked acolytes as they sheepishly slunk into view to stand by

93

his side like obedient pets. One held an old ghetto blaster and the other a portable dry-ice machine that he was desperately trying to turn off as he coughed as a result of the eschewing vapours.

"Allow me to introduce myself," the man of the cloth continued, ignoring his bumbling helpers. "My name is Alessio Varese, the Cardinal Camerlengo or the Pope's Official Assistant if you prefer the less formal title. I will be your host and guide during this televised show." At this point his assistants sniggered which elicited a glower from the Camerlengo. "Now, I am sure you all have many questions but first I have to relay some very important news to you that, due to your rushed journey here, you may not have heard. I am very pleased to announce that a new Pope has been elected!" The squat assistants clapped as if on cue but the Camerlengo was disappointed when he could see no discernible reaction from the young adults he faced. Not to worry, he thought. It would be their turn to be disappointed very soon! "Be rest assured though my children, although this endeavour was devised and organized solely by the late pontiff we will still be pressing ahead with the reality show despite the obvious heavy workload and undoubted different ambitions and goals of the new Pontiff. Now, follow me as we move on to your accommodation and I will explain how the show will work over the next few weeks." Rubbing his hands together as if trying to engender some enthusiasm in his bewildered guests he urged them to follow him through the dark doorway.

"Are we being filmed right now?" Asked a bright-eyed Alice.

"No. We will commence filming later on today in the public part of the museum. Obviously with the change of pope, the museums are currently closed to tourists so it is a good opportunity for that."

"Surely there will be more contestants than just us four though?" asked Dino, to nodded agreement from Alice.

"Oh yes!" The Camerlengo replied, lying through his teeth and hoping that the opposite would actually be the case. "Others will be joining at regular intervals over the next couple of weeks."

"What exactly is this show all about?" Asked a sanguine looking Laura. "The invitations we received gave very little information about it. Only that it would be the 'next big reality show' and a chance for 'heroic actions' but what does that all mean?"

"Ah! The best question so far my proverbial lambs! That is best answered in the public domain and straight to camera I would think so if you will all follow me, we can do exactly that and let the games begin!"

Beckoned by the Camerlengo, they all followed him into the dark space from whence he and his assistants had come, everyone keeping a safe distance from those odd-looking creatures at his side.

Of the four young men and women, only Luca did not share the excitement and curiosity that visibly pulsed from the others. Naturally a more cautious and reserved sort of person, he instead felt a burgeoning dread. He hoped that he was wrong but he couldn't help thinking that maybe everything was not quite as it seemed.

The prisoner looked at his watch, Swiss of course. He only had a few minutes before the mail train would be passing by so he left his fake house for the last time. He was glad finally to be taking some action instead of months of planning how to escape without being caught or killed and the same amount of time reminiscing about his earlier and simpler days in the Swiss Alps.

Switzerland was only his adopted country but he now loved it as if he had been born there, cherishing the memories of it like a father remembers the loving moments with an adopted son. He recalled the beautiful spring meadows of colourful flowers and the physical pursuits on those steep hillsides he had discovered, like the graceful sport of Hornussen. Now, with little else to do in his jail, he spent his time thinking about the adrenalin buzz he used to get from those short warm weeks in the spring when he enjoyed nothing more than slapping a small rubber oval with a huge flexible pole, sending it buzzing high and long into the clear mountain air. There was then the anxious wait to see if the opposing team had brought down the hornuss using their 'catching boards' as they flung them up into the sky, leaping like mad march hares. Slumped shoulders from the catchers would always mean the puck (or hornuss) had reached the ground first and valuable points for the batting team, the further it travelled the more they scored.

For many years he had also dreamed about going back to the places in Italy where he spent his early life but he knew it had not been possible. He knew his ego would not allow him to remain *incognito*. He would crave the ability to show off his powers and show his former works of art to a new generation but he knew that being seen as who he truly was would be to endanger his freedom.

But then, something changed. An opportunity for revenge presented itself and the truth could be revealed to the world. It may come at a cost but he was willing to risk the price of the renunciation. Unfortunately someone almost as powerful as him realized this opportunity at the same time and imprisoned him to take the prize all for himself. Not for much longer though thought the prisoner.

He was swiftly brought back to the present day as he heard a train's whistle in the hidden distance. He broke into a run, for once forgoing the risk of such movement being spotted during the day. Normally hordes of tourists would be watching but today, after the destruction he had wrought on the model, only the caretaker was present. In fact he was lucky that the trains were still running in the absence of paying guests as the lines were being checked for more hidden damage.

Leaving the front garden he galloped beside the narrow gravel road that snaked down from the hills and gradually nestled alongside the railway line. He used the scratchy green hedgerow for cover and dared not look up as he bolted towards the mail crane positioned a short distance before the next station. Upon reaching the crane he climbed its short height using the footholds provided and positioned himself where the mailbag would be. As he crouched precariously, he could already see the train approaching slowly from around the corner, its speed increasing gently as it headed onto the straight section of track.

Not waiting for the side arm on the train to harshly barge him into the carriage he jumped early, timing the leap to perfection. After a short roll he came to rest against the opposite interior of the dark mail truck. That morning, under cover of darkness, he had already changed the points on the track up ahead. The speed of the train at that point would be almost flat out and a crash would surely result.

The prisoner braced himself for the inevitable impact but he knew worse would be to follow as the train would leave the track and the hillside altogether, plunging off a steep drop. If he survived that he was sure he could escape and be free, even though he knew there were other perilous hurdles to successfully negotiate before he could reach his desired destination.

II-V – THE VATICAN MUSEUMS

The Camerlengo led his two assistants and four companions into the dark internal corridor that was now used for containing mops, buckets and spare light bulbs. In the past it would have served as a secret exit for the Pope and his acolytes to escape from invading forces. The last pontiff obviously didn't know of these passages though, or at least did not have time (or the desire) to use them to make good his escape before it was too late.

He beamed like the circus ringmaster he decided he needed to be at that moment but in truth he was nervous. He was winging it and that made him deeply uncomfortable. This day had been planned for years and nearly every eventuality had been permutated to eliminate risk of failure. However, he had certainly not expected four young people to turn up at a virtually unknown service door with wax-sealed invitations from the (now late) pope himself to participate in some sort of televised show! That wily old cad had obviously somehow figured out at least some of what he was planning and had tried to flood the Vatican with willing and able witnesses! How many of these invitations had the old man sent out he thought? Tens? Hundreds? Thousands? Oh well, now it mattered not mused the Camerlengo as only these four had turned up and these bright-eyed youngsters would easily be unwittingly corralled into an secure area out of the way and who knows, four hostages may even come in handy at some point. If the Pope thought an influx of young patriots were going to save him or the church he was utterly mistaken.

It was almost pitch black but the walk was short and the Camerlengo knew the way. He was now calmer but the muffled footsteps and excited whispers of the group behind him did make his heart skip faster. He could not wait to see the looks on their faces in a few moments time.

Another few steps and then he stopped, reaching out in the darkness and feeling for the wooden door he knew to be there. With a gentle push it swung soundlessly inwards, the mechanism still working effortlessly after so many centuries, a mark of fine Renaissance workmanship that could not or would not be replicated today. A golden light flooded into the gloomy space, bouncing off small particles of ancient dust as they danced through the air.

The Camerlengo stepped out into the light with an air of unwarranted grace, followed by his ungainly assistants and finally the quartet of bounding young adults. "Welcome to the Vatican museums, my especially invited guests," the Camerlengo began as he trod confidently across the marble floored room. "I say 'museums' in the plural as there are many under these roofs and not just one as you will shortly see. Here we have emerged into the *Museo Pio-Clementino* near the start of the tour. In this hallway we have a fine collection of ancient statues, collected over the last 500 years." The long room contained a series of identical arches along each side, every one housing a different statue in its recess, placed on a pedestal like a huge chess piece.

"I apologize for your unusual entrance to the museums but the...um...television show we are making with your help must be executed with no external interference. To that end, once I show you to the rooms where you will be filmed, you will of course be locked away from the outside world. Once you are safely ensconced you will be secure. I am sure I don't need to remind you that the Vatican museums are probably the most protected sets of buildings in the world. Nothing and nobody can leave here without the knowledge of myself as I am the Camerlengo. Now, if you would like to follow me this way, I will show you the rest of the museums before you begin your show."

"Can we not just go straight to the Sistine chapel and miss out on all this other stuff?" posed Dino, who feared the onset of boredom very soon.

"I am afraid not my child," replied the powerful priest. "I will need the time during which we tour in order to explain to you the rules of the game show to you. However, as we are the only people here the tour will be considerably quicker than a normal day." He smiled a patronizing smile in the manner of an experienced doctor dismissing the point of an unknowledgeable patient.

Onward the small gang pressed, following their guide who continued to explain various points of interest along the route. It was a journey through time bookmarked by room after room of impressive ancient artefacts that were gradually replaced by newer and more recent antiquities. In *the museo Egiziano* they marvelled at sarcophagi of Egyptian pharaohs long since turned to dust before cantering through decades at a time in the Etruscan era brought to life with archaeological finds of ancient Greece and Rome. Finally, they reached The Gallery of Maps that marked the start of the Renaissance period. Here, the Camerlengo explained, was a topographical representation of the whole of Italy, depicted beautifully in over a hundred huge paintings, commissioned in the 16th century.

By now however the Camerlengo's ever florid descriptions were falling on deaf ears. The two girls were beginning to fatigue after their long journeys, wondering when they would be reunited with their cases of clothes, make-up and other effects they had brought with them. The Neapolitan Dino was daydreaming. He had spent the first half of the walk to date thinking about the net worth of all the valuables around him, fantasizing at being able to own and (more importantly sell) even one of these near-priceless works of art. Thoughts of wealth then turned to his other great passion as he made the most of the two girls being distracted. Deliberately dropping back a few meters, he allowed his eyes to gorge on the feast of fine female flesh in front of him. He mused that he could happily spend hours mentally debating the contrasting merits of a body-hugging pair of jeans (worn by Alice) verses an equally restrictive dress (sported by Laura).

Alice's choice of attire was at first more appealing he considered. Her legs were snugly encased underneath the tight denim, every subtle curve displayed as if the malleable blue material was her skin itself. In contrast, Laura's three-quarter length dress meant Dino had to use his imagination more which, in his case, was never a bad thing in his opinion. There was also something more mesmerizing and tantalizing about the synchronous way her high-heeled feet moved forward in a staccato but sinuous wave of movement, showing first one bare calf and then the next, the extra inches in her heel used not just to gain height but also for added definition in her slender leg muscles.

Walking slightly behind the rest, but for a very different reason to Dino, was Luca. He was even more distracted than the others and frankly, had been quite concerned from the outset. He could not quite figure out why he felt wary but he knew that somehow this odd little private tour around the empty museums was beginning to make less and less sense. Then, by seeing something out the large windows in the Gallery of Maps, he decided he had gathered enough evidence to quiz the Camerlengo on a couple of matters.

"My Camerlengo…," the Venetian started unsurely.

"Please, call me Cam," he replied.

Luca paused but decided not to be overly familiar, thought about using the odd moniker but politely declined. "My Camerlengo, May I ask you a couple of questions please?"

"Of course! What would a guide be if he couldn't answer an enquiry from his visitor! Are you interested in the pope that commissioned these fine works of art? Or perhaps you would like to know more about how the paintings were made?" He hoped not as he did not know the answers and cared even less. Thankfully they were now near the secure rooms where he could reveal all, once these sacrificial lambs were penned in.

"No. I would like to ask firstly about the statues…"

"Yes?...Yes!" He responded with wide eyes and fake enthusiasm.

"Why do they have tags tied to their toes or fingers? And why do many of these tags appear to have names and addressed inscribed with a price in Euros?"

A flash of anger appeared to cross the face of the Camerlengo but he regained his composure almost instantly. He had been expecting this question after all. "Oh that is nothing of real interest. The tags are on statues and other works of art that require remedial repairs, cleaning and such like. The addresses are where they need to be sent for the work to be done. Hence why some are already wrapped up, ready to go."

"And the prices?"

"You make it look like we are planning some sort of garage sale here Mr. Luca!" Everyone chuckled at this seemingly preposterous notion, apart from Luca himself. "The price tags are what each piece needs to be insured against damage in transit to and from the restorers. Now, if that is all, we really must be getting on. You cannot be late for the first live show after all!"

As the last words of the Camerlengo finished echoing around the ornate marbled surrounds, the unperturbed Luca asked one more question. "Fair enough, but why are there so many Swiss Guards present in the courtyard?" he replied, pointing outside the large barred windows.

The whole group turned to look outside to where he was pointing. The quadrant below was filled by a throng of the Swiss Guards in their familiar colourful tunics. A whole regiment was present, split into groups of twenty men, each occupying a discrete section of the paved enclosure. Each score of soldiers were practicing a different aspect of fitness or warfare. As some speared dummies filled with sand that swung helplessly on chains, others engaged in fierce hand-to-hand combat. Whilst one small cabal concentrated on gymnastic feats others shot targets with pistols from many yards distant. At this sight, Luca's companions visibly showed some concern, disturbed by the clear show of force below them.

Again, the Camerlengo was quick to try and dismiss their fears. "Please, do not be worried by such acts. Every time a new Pope is chosen, the guards perform a private show of their skills for the new pontiff. Hundreds of years ago it would have shown the Pope that he was well protected. Today, of course, it is merely tradition. Today you see them all practicing for the inauguration ceremony tomorrow. That is all, I promise. Now, let us move on to the crowning glory which I am sure you have all been dying to see…The Sistine Chapel!"

Luca remained unconvinced by the Camerlengo's explanations but he knew any further queries would probably be quashed by his peers who were now all excited by the thought of seeing Michelangelo's masterpiece painted onto the walls and ceilings of the ancient chapel without the inconvenience of being crowded by hundreds of other tourists.

102

After a short walk down a rather narrow and unassuming staircase, everyone passed through the average looking door and on into the decidedly less than average chapel beyond. With everyone now safely inside and with each craned neck looking up at the intricate mural, the Camerlengo reached into his pocket to secretly press a button on a hidden fob he carried. All too engrossed in the ancient marvel, nobody noticed all the exits being sealed silently by thick steel doors that slid over the openings from hidden housings within the wall cavities. Now that he finally had them where he wanted them, the Camerlengo was grateful he could drop his placating and friendly act.

"Right you ragamuffins, gather round," he said, roughly gesticulating to the young adults who were surprised by his change of tone and manner but acquiesced all the same.

"Now, I have a few things to tell you which will come as a surprise," he continued with more than a smudge of malice. "What you all know is that we have a new pope. What you *don't* know is that he is merely a puppet for a tyrannical billionaire turned eccentric warlord and we killed all the other papal candidates to ensure our guy would be successful".

At this confession, the visitors (apart from Luca) all laughed, convinced that this was all part of the show.

"Oh and you are not part of a game show, there is no game show, no cameras, no prize, no adoring public, nothing. The invitations you received were a ruse by the old pope before he died. I think he hoped to attract active young people like yourselves to the Vatican so he could reveal what we were planning and that you would somehow save the Vatican and Christendom. Unfortunately for him, and yourselves, we killed him before you arrived. We could have turned you away but we thought a few hostages might be useful if things didn't go to plan."

The room reverberated with nervous laughs at the ridiculous plot. Luca still wasn't amused though. At last Dino managed to control his mirth for long enough to join in with what he supposed were just high jinks. "And I suppose those tags on the statues and paintings really were price tags and you are going to sell everything to the highest bidders?"

"Yes, exactly right," replied the Camerlengo, matter-of-factly. "For example, just this morning we agreed the sale of a rather fine statue of the Roman emperor Augustus to a Texan oil baron!"

By this point the three laughing visitors were almost doubled-over with merriment that was becoming contagious, the Camerlengo's two henchmen chuckling away, even if they weren't exactly sure why.

"And I bet these guns are real too!" said Dino sarcastically, tears of joy falling from his eyes as he grabbed a pistol from the loose hands of one of the squat assistants, pointing it towards the floor before the greasy creature could regain the weapon. Brandishing the gun casually, more like a banana than a firearm, Dino pulled the trigger. All laughter ceased as the bullet exploded from the gun, sounding more like a cannon ball in the enclosed space of the chapel. Before anyone else could recover, the Camerlengo snatched back the weapon and retained it himself before pointing it squarely in the direction of the now startled quartet.

"Yep, sorry chaps, the party is over but please feel free to make the most of your spacious surroundings for the time being, until I work out what to do with you. I will get my assistants to bring your things in shortly so at least you will have some "creature comforts" during your stay. Until the next time my subjects, I bid you arrivederci!" With that the Camerlengo turned and walked towards one of the exits, pressing another button on the plipper in his pocket to open up a solitary door in the far wall.

As Dino was still shocked from the gun being real it was up to Laura to be a voice of defiance. "You won't get away with it! The prime minister of Italy and his armed forces will soon be here to rescue us, his Italian citizens!"

"I wouldn't bet on it my dear," said the Camerlengo without bothering to turn to face her. "He would not lift a finger unless it benefits him personally and besides, nobody even knows you are here!"

The door locked firmly shut behind the three plotting churchmen as a cloak of doom and fear descended on those left inside. Individually they all knew he was right. It was a stipulation of their invitations that they told nobody of their participation. They had been seen to enter the Vatican by some of the journalists earlier but would they know or care who they were? Even if they did they would probably never dream they were in such plight before it was too late.

The woe of the four companions mirrored that of the agonized souls on the walls behind them as they came to terms with their imprisonment in one of the most famous places in the world, hoping the infamously selfish leader of their country would somehow learn of their fate and effect their rescue.

The old man wearily lifted his bulk a few inches off the baking sun bed, adjusting his small swimming trunks to ensure as much of his body would be exposed to the fierce sun as possible without quite uncovering his shrivelled genitalia.

The young woman squatting beside him sighed for two reasons. Firstly because of the sickening sound as he lifted his sticky and sweat-drenched body from the synthetic canvas (akin to fresh wallpaper peeling off a wall when too much paste had been applied) and secondly because she was trying to perform the delicate task of plucking his errant eyebrows at the time.

On the other side of the wrinkly pensioner, a nubile and barely-clothed girl lazily fanned him with a huge palm leaf and a bored expression.

Behind the pampered prone figure, his personal assistant (the only other male visible in the secluded and very well protected small beach) read out the sun burnt man's itinerary for the remainder of the day. "Well after the eyebrow plucking we must return inside, sir, for your consultation with the hair specialist."

"Ah, yes," said the old man, instinctively touching his thinning bonce. "Please remember to prepare my bandana for when he has finished. You know how sore my head gets after each treatment. I looked like a beetroot last time in front of the King of Wales!"

"That would be the Prince of Wales your excellence, but otherwise, very true."

"I knew that you fool!" he spat, a flailing arm hitting the palm leaf that swayed by his side, the lothario shrieking as his wayward hand received a paper cut from one of the sharp fronds. "What else have I got on today?" he demanded, now with a sour expression that doubled the wrinkles on his forehead as he sucked on his bleeding digit to stem the flow.

"Well, my liege I am afraid after that we should really address some pressing work matters."

"Why do you always have to bother me with these trifling things? Leave any documents on my desk to sign as usual and if a statement is required just say we are "in support" or "we do not condone", blah, blah, blah. The opposite of whatever we said last time. I am on holiday after all for goodness sake!"

Now, no longer relaxed and irritated by the thought of work, the saggy old man roused himself from his seat, beckoning both his female aids to put his dressing gown on for him, slapping each one on their derrieres as they walked away.

The assistant jogged after him. "I'm afraid it is not that simple sir as it appears a rather difficult diplomatic situation is in progress. You see, the Vatican has been taken over by a Swiss maniac and the western world are pressing us to take control of the situation."

"Fine, fine," he said dismissively as he climbed onto his motorized golf buggy that would take him the twenty yards back to his palatial summer house. "I guess I will have to make a statement on this and the army can take control and do whatever they think is best. Cut off all ties with Switzerland, ban their cheese, clocks, that sort of thing. That should do it." Conversation over as far as he was concerned, he sped off up the beach only to slam on the brakes half way home. Turning back to face his assistant, he barked one more question. "Hold on. Where do I keep all my secret personal finances?"

"Switzerland, sir."

"Ah…Maybe it's best to wait and see what happens for a couple of days. It wouldn't do to be too hasty now would it."

"Yes, prime minister. As you wish prime minister."

II-VII – THE VATICAN (ST. PETER'S BASILICA)

To call St. Peter's Basilica a church is akin to calling the blue whale a fish. Its dimensions are vast and as if to prove (or boast) the point, the length of other great churches and cathedrals from around the world are marked by small bronze plaques well within its 730 feet length. St. Paul's Cathedral, for example, would easily fit inside with over 200 feet to spare. The proportions of the Vatican church are also considered aesthetically beautiful as its length is 1.618 times its height, the so-called 'golden ratio' that so fascinated the renaissance scholars at the time it was built.

Similarly, to call the St. Peter's Basilica gift shop (situated on the flat roof beneath the great dome) a tatty souvenir shop would be like calling Harrods a pound store. However, like its less venerable counterparts, it is true that this shop *does* sell souvenirs, even if its goods are of a much higher quality than the norm and staffed solely by nuns. That day, in that most unusual of gift shops, the nuns were making the most of the absence of visitors due to the papal change by using the time to apparently perform a stock-take.

It might seem strange to find a gift shop in such a holy location and indeed when souvenir shops had first sprung up outside the city walls in the 1960's the church had vociferously shunned their commercial practices and sinful use of the image of Christ on their products. However, after a couple of decades of observing the money spinning opportunities of such tat, the church famously performed a complete u-turn. And so the small shop on top of the basilica that used to sell only Vatican state stamps and postcards was transformed into a glitzy den of religious tourist souvenirs with every possible pilgrim need catered for from within its cramped confines.

This souvenir shop did not need to advertise but if it did you could imagine the type of sales patter that would be employed, for example, on a television advert.

Need to show your love of Jesus as you walk the streets proclaiming his good name? Then why not wear your colours on your chest by choosing from our wide range of t-shirts and sweat-shirts depicting the image of Our Lord in a range of popular poses including the best-selling "winking/thumbs up" print or maybe just a simple "I heart JC" motif.

Having trouble reaching God with your prayers? Try our porcelain praying hands that will help to channel your messages up to heaven. And if you like to pray in the dark, why not see the light with our brand new glow in the dark crucifixes and Virgin Mary statuettes!

Has praying given you bleeding knees? Are your feet blistered after a long pilgrimage? Let Jesus heal you with sticking plasters that bare his caring face!

The stock take finished abruptly as the nuns saw the Swiss Guards on the roof sauntering off for their long lunch. The ruse over with, the clipboards clattered to the floor as the manager of the shop, the most senior nun in the Vatican, sprinted outside, hitching up her habit to avoid tripping. Skipping past the lines of curved white railings on the smooth rust coloured roof, she almost skidded to a halt next to a small circular enclosure that resembled an over-sized and overly-ornate telephone booth. Safely inside, she pulled a hidden lever on the floor and began to descend into the dark wall cavity of the basilica.

II-VIII – THE VATICAN (SISTINE CHAPEL)

As the setting sun sunk beneath the unseen horizon its last rays of light left the chapel along with the hope of its unwilling occupants. They greeted the sudden greyness of dusk with silence, small talk long having been exhausted, allowing fear and uncertainty to resurface to the fore-front of their minds. Grotesque figures on the frescoed walls surrounding them began to take on a more menacing façade as the settling gloom and lengthening shadows made their arms appear to reach out from the plaster towards the hostages pleading to be saved from perennial damnation in hell.

The temperature now began to drop noticeably, prompting Laura to reach into her handbag for warmer clothing. At this moment she was glad to have some creature comforts in her possession.

For the last hour Dino had sat away from the others, crouched by the door, waiting for the muscular but stupid assistants to make good their promise to reunite them with their bags. He had hoped to leap on them as they threw their possessions inside, incapacitating the bumbling duo and escaping past their dazed bulbous forms. Without warning a door did indeed then open but their bags were thrown in from another unseen secreted opening in the opposite wall. The door was closed again before any of them had a chance to move even a muscle in that direction. Dino returned crestfallen to the others as they instinctively huddled together in the middle of the vast space, silent and devoid of ideas.

Dino was never comfortable during periods of calm (as his teachers from his truncated period of education would testify) and he was the first to pierce the noiseless vacuum with his booming voice. "My friends," he started as he leapt up in front of the forlorn others, suddenly as eager as a young car salesman. "Let us not pray on thoughts of doom and gloom and lets distract ourselves by way of a discussion. Does anyone have any ideas for a topic?" Secretly he hoped they did not so he could proffer his own sordid suggestion. Sadly he was to be disappointed.

"What about religion? Seeing as we are all stuck in here, the very home of the catholic church," suggested Luca.

110

"Yes, not bad," replied Dino with condescension he barely bothered to hide. "Although I was thinking something more like s…"

"…So, Christianity," Laura interrupted, cutting off Dino with a cheeky grin as she starred him down, guessing what he was about to say and not wishing to encourage the testosterone-fuelled oik. "Why don't you kick us off *terrone*?"

Dino acted like he was shot in the heart by this mild insult commonly aimed at people from the south of Italy. (*'Terrone'* literally meaning 'dirty' and 'of the earth', was a slur used by some northerners against their southern cousins who are seen by some as nothing more than a bunch of poor peasant farmers by their generally more affluent and industrialized cousins. "Fine. Christianity it is! So then, shall we start with the holy book itself? Who here believes what it says?"

Alice was barely listening, preferring to perform some yoga moves of which a contortionist would be proud. The conversation was beginning to pique her interest though and she replied clearly, despite her head being between her legs. "I was always taught as a young child to believe every word in the Bible as the word of God but I started to doubt that as I grew older."

"Great start Alice!" said Dino, now pointing at her like a chat show host. "Well, let us look at the evidence. If we followed the great book to the letter you would, for example, have to believe that the world was made in six days and God rested on the Sunday. And because God rested on the Sabbath then everyone else should too. In fact it clearly states that anyone who works on that day should have to be put to death. That would mean the death to all footballers in *Serie A* for a start!"

"You can't take it that literally obviously," said Luca. "If we did then we would have to believe the world was only six and half thousand years old and dinosaurs never existed. It was just a way that scholars of the time could explain the creation of the universe and evolution to simple people who would not understand or believe the complexity of the actual situation."

"I think the bible is no different to modern society," said Laura vehemently. "It's just another method of state control. By making people believe in an all powerful and often vehement God it kept people in fear, damped their personal drive and allowed them to be controlled by their tribal leaders. At least it meant modern society could flourish."

"I believe it is more simple than that," Luca interjected. "It is true that the idea of a God is linked to fear but its more about the fear of the individual who cannot cope with the burden of their own intelligence compared to the rest of the animal kingdom. The vast majority of people cannot deal with the idea that we are in control of our own lives, our own destinies. We need to cling onto the notion that there is some other being or indeed beings who actually determine our fate leaving us more free to make those big life-changing decisions with reduced stress, carrying the belief that an outside force will actually decide our paths on this mortal coil. Name any society that there has ever been in the world and you will see a God or Gods. This is especially true of any group of people that were very advanced for their time. The more insecure they felt due to their position as the leaders of the known world, the more gods they had to make decisions for them. The ancient Greeks had about a dozen deities, the Egyptians – twenty and the Romans worshipped well over two hundred guarding almost every aspect of their lives!"

"You talk of control?" said Laura. "Surely where we are now is the greatest example of that?" she said, arcing her arm to highlight the frescos on the ceiling that they could now hardly see in the diminishing light.

"Ah, yes!" said Dino, rubbing his hands with glee. "I was wondering when we would come onto the specifics. The Catholic Church, the single most controlling organization in the world. Hundreds of millions of members who have their lives tracked through their confession of sins and their communication to God limited through his representatives, the priests. Moreover, at its head we have the Pope, a modern day, living, breathing, speaking version of the bible. No, actually more than that – a living mouthpiece for God and the same people who even today follow every word in the good book also follow his every word and instruction. And from power and control of their believers, they gain their trust and, more importantly, their money."

Alice was beginning to look angered by Dino's diatribe. "So do you think anyone that believes in God is simple and the church is just a money making corporation?"

Dino considered her point. "Not simple but perhaps weak-willed," he replied.

"Do you not have your own gods Dino?" Alice spat back. "The ones that play on the football field perhaps?"

The *terrone* laughed heartily before answering. "It may be true I worship them sometimes but I know they are not in control of my destiny, only my happiness. I know they don't walk on water like Jesus claimed to do".

"So you denounce his miracles too?" she said testily.

"Yes, I do as a matter of fact. I am sure many of those fantastic stories are works of complete fiction. They would have been written down by scholars hundreds of years after Jesus lived and the tales would only have been elaborated on as they were being passed down verbally through the generations, each new branch of the family tree adding their own guild to each golden story like Chinese whispers in a playground. After all, everyone likes a good story. I am sure there are grains of truth in a few of the tales but my own theory is that Jesus was a man from another country who arrived in Judea one day with a bag full of charm, charisma and a few sorcerer's tricks that won over the crowds like any other street performer. A well-meaning trickster that, for some reason, history has twisted into some sort of other worldly creature. Mind you, I wish he was here now though to turn some water into wine!"

"Hallelujah!" shouted Luca, making the others laugh, apart from Alice.

"I used to believe everything," she angrily shouted at the Neapolitan. "When I was a young girl I was deeply religious and so proud when my brother had the 'calling' to join the church. But I lost all faith when he was hounded out of the priesthood for allegedly getting too close to one of the nuns. It was all lies though. He told me the real reason was because he wasn't bringing in enough money from his congregation each Sunday on the collection plate."

Luca was the next to pipe up. "I also had the faith when I was a boy. I even went to Sunday school every week but I ripped up my hymnbook when I was ten years old because I was angry with God. How could He have allowed my pet hamster to die I thought. Stupid I know, but at the time it was what turned me away from Christianity."

"It had me under a spell for a time too," Laura commented. "But I guess God just became less important in my life as other things took its place."

"Like me?" said Dino suggestively.

Laura narrowed her eyes. "Don't push your luck volcano boy!" she replied.

Despite the dig, Dino wondered if he saw a softening in Laura's attitude towards him but it was not easy to tell as he doubted anyone was acting normally or thinking straight due to their unexpected incarceration. "It might surprise you all to learn that I too was a devoted Christian in my younger days. I was even an obedient altar boy!"

Everyone laughed at the mental image of a well-behaved Dino in his Sunday best, handling the wafers for communion.

"I bet you were a cute little boy" said Laura, making Dino's spirits jump a little and Luca's sink. The Venetian could see the predictable game of the alpha male taming the alpha female yet again in an intricate but transparent dance in which he so rarely participated.

"So what went wrong?" asked a curious Alice of Dino, "What is your tale?"

"Some would say what went *right* Laura! I too got interested in other things as I grew up…and at first it was the money on the collection plate!"

"You stole from the church?!" said Laura with mock shock.

"Doesn't the church steal from us?" replied Dino. "Maybe I was just taking back from the rich to give to the poor…e.g. me!"

"Well it appears they have certainly taken us," added Luca thoughtfully.

With that, a melancholic air descended once again over the group. Trying to suppress his own fears with more game play, Dino turned his attention back to thoughts that more often filled his head as he sidled up to Laura. "Do not fear *carina*" he said as she nervously edged away, "I will find a way to get us out of here if it's the last thing we do."

"It may well be the last thing *you* do if you don't move away from me!" she replied.

Clearly more time was needed to warm up this thawing frozen maiden thought Dino. At least time was something that appeared to be an abundant commodity.

Luca sniggered at Dino's rejection by the demure Laura, heartened that the brash and bold did not always get their way.

"Hey, quiet boy, less of the laughter!" Dino said with hurt pride as he turned on the Venetian. "I am just trying to protect these fine young ladies as you sit there doing nothing!"

Alice answered for him as she strode over to join the conversation from where she had been performing yoga. "Don't you worry about us. We can look after ourselves thank you very much."

"Ok, ok. Point taken girls! I will leave you both and Luca to fend for yourselves. In the mean time I will continue to look for a way to escape on my own and then you will be rid of me," he said with more than a hint of mocked self-pity. "I am sure there will be another exit here somewhere…Perhaps in the floor this time?" He rushed to his right a few steps and squealed in fake revelation. "Ah, maybe here?" he said, stamping his right foot down on a triangle pattern within the mosaic floor. "Or maybe even here?" Again, his foot came crashing down on a series of swirling white lines in the small tiles.

At first the others had sniggered but quickly lost interest in his very amateur dramatics and looked away. Thus they did not see an arc of light trace a perfect circle around the spot where Dino now stood. It was only when the circle began to fill with light that he silently moved away in instinctive fear. And he was soon glad he had as the area now rose from the floor as a disc supported by four slender metallic columns. The eminence and the gushing sound of the elevating platform alerted the others to this bizarre and unexpected sight. When the disc was two feet from the ground, a shrouded female head began to emerge, rising up like a subterranean worker returning to street level through an open manhole. The four hostages instinctively crossed themselves. Despite their varying degrees of receded belief in the creator they all thought they may need Him on their side for the next few moments.

II-IX – MILANO TO ROMA

Mice were rife once more at the central postal office in Rome. That was the only conclusion the postal master could arrive at when he was presented with a strange empty package to inspect.

It appeared the package had burst open from the inside. Therefore he surmised that the only possible explanation was that the small rodent must have entered the padded envelope through a corner that had not been affixed properly by the sender and then later, no doubt in a panic, gnawed his way out straight through the side of the large padded envelope at some point on route. The burly man shuddered at the prospect, not being a fan of rodents. There was one other peculiar aspect of this item of post though. The address on the exterior had been written from right and left and back to front.

Puzzled but intrigued, the postal master placed a mirror against the text and peered into the silver-backed sheet of glass. He read the corrected image he saw and entered the name of the street into an internet search engine. The result showed the *strada* in question had indeed once existed but it had been demolished over three hundred years ago. Shaking his head at the strange ways of folk he tossed the ruined envelope into the bin, not seeing a tiny shoe flying out the opening.

Outside the back of the sorting office, a bruised and dishevelled looking man slunk into the encroaching night of the dark side streets. He quickly found a deserted cul-de-sac and huddled inside a large discarded cardboard box. He was content to sleep in squalor that night as it meant no one would come looking for him here. He laughed quietly to himself as he remembered the damp artist's workshop floors he had slept on in the past. Some were worse than this with rotten food and plagued with rats, although he had to admit to himself that had been a very long time ago, several lifetimes for some. He fell asleep, looking forward to the day he had planned tomorrow and the surprised look he would create on the faces of certain people he would be about to meet.

II-X – THE VATICAN (SISTINE CHAPEL)

Not for the first time that day, the group of four young adults found themselves unavoidably paralyzed by fear. On this occasion, due to a ghostly figure rising up from beneath a solid floor that now appeared to have hidden facets. With nothing to defend themselves against this new and possibly hostile intruder they were defenceless as the apparition stepped out from its unusual elevator and walked towards them.

Dino sank to his knees to worship the being. "Mother Mary!" he wailed. "Forgive me my sins and my wayward path from the church. Please help us in this, our hour of need!"

The figure looked down at the supplicant. "Get up you fool. I may be a mother…a mother *superior* but my name is certainly *not* Mary!"

As the figure came closer, her shadow engulfed them all and within the umbra they could discern more definition in what was now clearly a very real middle-aged nun with a kind but serious looking face.

"Oh well," said Dino as he righted himself and brushed himself down. "I've found it's always best to hedge your bets in life."

The holy lady smiled thinly. "There is only one path to salvation my child, you should know that well enough. Now all of you quickly follow me into the elevator whilst I explain a few things." Without hesitating, the holy woman stepped back onto the circular platform, leaving space for the others to squeeze in next to her. It was only when she turned around that she saw they had not budged one iota.

"What is the matter with you? You don't trust nuns?"

Once again Dino responded for the group. "Well we thought we could trust the Pope's assistant and look where that has left us!"

With a softer look the Nun responded. "Very well. I can appreciate this has been a difficult situation for you all so I will leave you with this choice. You can either stay here locked in this cold, dark room at the will of the Camerlengo and the new Pope or you can follow me. If you do the latter I think, in time, I can get you all out of here."

Laura looked shocked. "In time?!" We want to get out of here now!"

"I wish I could help you quicker but I'm afraid it will not be simple to get you out too hastily. The whole of the Vatican has been cut off from the outside world and there are only two options left to get out, both of which are unlikely to succeed and fraught with dangers. Your best chance is if the Italian army storms the Vatican, then you can be rescued and freed. The trouble is I cannot see that happening anytime soon as we are an independent state and that would amount to invading foreign soil. I fear they would rather lay siege and starve out the twisted Camerlengo, his puppet Pope and the Swiss guards and that could take months with the stockpiles of food we have here".

Luca echoed the others thoughts with his question. "And what pray tell, what is the second option?"

The nun paused before answering in a lowered, more considered voice. "That I cannot explain myself but I can take you to a man who can. It certainly should be quicker but the chance of failure is high".

When a lab rat is trapped in an unfamiliar room, it will nearly always move through a door when it opens, even though it has no knowledge of what might lay beyond. And it was with this sentiment the quartet followed the nun onto the glowing circle and its confined open elevator and then downwards into the unknown.

Dino had always suffered from mild claustrophobia so being in a small open lift that was descending through solid rock to goodness knows where was not the ideal situation for him. At least the cramped environment allowed him to be within a couple of inches of Laura without her being able to object. Her height advantage over him also had another benefit - his eye line at her chest level. He was not sure what was more intoxicating - the ever so gentle curve of her cleavage, a sumptuous shallow valley that disappeared into a dark promised land beneath the top of her dress or the captivating smell of her perfume, still radiating its vapour from the heat of her body. He felt his heart beat faster until he sensed the object of his desire was watching him. Automatically he looked up to Laura's face where her raised eyebrows and tight-lipped mouth showed she was not amused by his obvious mental undressing. He turned his head away, smiling as he felt his cheeks tighten as they visibly reddened. What was it about this woman that disarmed him so much? He had only just met her and she was just the latest visceral object of desire, the last in a long line of similar girls he had chased in his life. But no, something *was* different here. He felt somehow that she was the one in control, the one with the power between them. He knew he was heading into uncharted waters and as this unsettling feeling began to manifest itself with a fluttering in his stomach he wished for a distraction until he could sort out what was going on with his normally reliable paper-thin intentions. As the open elevator violently jerked within the narrow cavity he had his wish as it reminded him of his fear of enclosed spaces once more.

The cage continued on its cavernous journey that had now lasted a couple of minutes or more. Alice was nervous. She was used to being in complete control of what she was doing and when she did it. Today that right had been taken away from her. Forlornly she took her mobile out of her bag. She knew there would be no signal, but she looked anyway. The battery would not last much longer and she knew she should turn it off in case she had the opportunity to try to use it later but somehow she couldn't do it as she hated the idea of not being able to be contacted. It would be just her luck that her agent would try to call today with some good news for once she thought, preferring to focus on her evaporating career aspirations rather than the notions of another life growing inside her. Sorrowfully and carefully, as if putting a baby to bed, she rested her phone back in her bag to sleep. Luca tried to focus his mind on nothing but the roughly hewn rock that crept past as they descended into the bowels of the earth. He was again regretting leaving the comfort of Venice. He may not have been happy with his life and his work but at least he had had a good wage and a relatively easy life. He frowned as he considered what he had swapped that life for - an uncertain journey, probably with a perilous end in the company of two headstrong women and a testosterone-filled idiot. He sighed quietly but it was still loud enough for the nun who stood beside him to hear.

120

"Just a few seconds now," she said in a voice so calming that it could only be possessed by someone at great inner peace and great faith in otherworldly benefactors. "In fact, here we are!" she said triumphantly as the dark rough walls gave way to a pitch-black curtain of space, the lift juddering to a halt. Despite a deep desire for space and the comforting feeling of *terra firma*, the complete absence of light ensured the occupants of the elevator remained staunchly in place, suddenly preferring the devil they knew.

Reaching out into the darkness, the nun felt along a wall that could not be seen. "Where are those damned lights," she muttered, unaware of her blasphemy. "Ah, here they are," she said with relief.

Some ten metres ahead of them, suspended from a ceiling of the same height, a single reluctant bulb blinked sleepily before finally remaining illuminated with some apparent unwillingness. The strength of the glow was weak but its luminosity increased gradually as everyone adjusted their eyes to the low light.

"I do hate these new-fangled energy saving light bulbs," said the nun casually. "I know we are meant to be saving God's world but I wish they were a little more powerful…Anyway, follow me my children." The nun led them into the centre of the light's etendue as everyone shiftily cast their eyes around their new surroundings. They were in the corner of a white basement room with a ceiling as high as a house and walls that were brilliantly white but completely bare.

In front of them stood an enormous bookcase that stretched from floor to ceiling with long metal shelves suspended between the uprights. Each sturdy layer bulged with boxes and files of various shapes, sizes and conditions. Some were made of cardboard and had obviously been placed there in recent times whereas others had been resting longer, such as some large leather-bounded and metal studded travelling cases, covered in thick layers of dust. More ancient looking still were the bundles of yellowing scrolls that incongruously sat next to smaller artefacts such as colourful vases and statuettes. Despite the apparent haphazard hoarding, everything on the shelves appeared to be catalogued, either with notated coloured tags tied on with string or small sticky labels.

121

At the foot of these immense shelving units, mattresses covered in duvets had been laid on the bare floor with a large boxes of edible provisions at one end. As the others gazed in tired bewilderment, Dino voiced his opinion angrily. "What is this? Do you expect us to sleep here and eat like common pigs out of a box? We want you to show us the exit now. We have all had enough of these games!"

The nun looked a little sad. "I wish I could let you leave but all the exits are patrolled by the Camerlengo and his Swiss Guards tonight. The only way you can leave is to use what resources we have here, buried deep in this vast room, but I must ask you all to feed, drink and rest. I trust you will be relatively comfortable here and I will return in the morning."

Laura stepped forward now to challenge the holy sister. "Are you saying you are going to leave us alone here in this huge dark cellar?"

"Please believe me, it is the safest place for you all tonight," replied the nun. "I can understand how difficult it must be for you to rest in these current circumstances so I will help you out in that regard." Before anyone could ask the nun what she meant, she produced a small mask from her pocket and placed it over her nose and mouth before moving back towards the wall by the light switch where she pushed a small red button. A hissing sound filled the air and within a couple of seconds the four young adults were unconscious, falling safely onto the mattresses at their feet. Keeping the mask firmly against her face, the nun stepped back into the elevator and left the basement.

II-XI – THE STREETS OF ROME

The dishevelled man had spent a night under a cardboard box but he still awoke with happiness and vigour as overnight he had regained enough strength to magically return to his former stature. Looking up from the dark alleyway to the sky above he was heartened that it was blue. He wasted no time in stepping out from the shadows and into the warmth of the main streets.

He guessed it must be the time of the morning rush hour as the pedestrainised road was a throng of jostling people moving in both directions as they rushed past him. He felt like a stone in the way of two lines of opposing ants busily going about their urgent business. The bustling creatures only stopped to shuffle left or right past someone coming the other way and everyone ignored the strange unkempt man.

He did not want anyone to see him and attract the unwanted attention that it would bring. To ensure that no curious or well-meaning individuals came too close, he exerted a little mental control over anyone who engaged in eye contact. The effort to do this for too many or too long was draining though and he knew he would need to seek quieter thoroughfares before very long.

He did need to be noticed by one of these plebeians though and the next candidate he saw was perfect for his nefarious needs. An obese man, grown fat on his own unethically sustained wealth, wobbled directly towards him. The dishevelled man stood still, exactly in his path so that the well-dressed man would have to look at him before he chose to lurch to the left or the right to pass. The dishevelled man looked directly into his heavy eyes and without hesitation the fat man reached into his pocket and handed over his wallet before moving on his way. Casually the dishevelled man sauntered on as he plucked out the valuable banknotes before throwing the wallet back over his shoulder. Unconsciously the fat man turned back, picked up his wallet and moved on. Later on that day he would blame a clever pickpocket for lightening his purse, pleased that his credit cards were still there and he had been saved the inconvenience of calling his secretary to cancel his cards for him. He would not miss a few hundred Euros, small change to a man of his means.

The dishevelled man now saw his chosen route had been a propitious one. He was on a street filled with clothes shops and other haberdashers. Stepping confidently into one of the more flamboyant looking establishments, he used a modicum of mental control over the staff to ignore his unusual attire that would normally have resulted in a speedy ejection. The sight of the large wedge of bank notes in his hand was also a strong lure to the greedy shopkeeper. Times change but money still talks louder than many voices he thought.

Within the hour he was fitted out in a new suit of a rich purple hue (always the colour of the more important people in society, regardless of the era) complete with well fitting shoes made from alligator hide. Stepping back out onto the main street he now invited looks from the passers-by. He required one last stop before he could head west to The Vatican and stepped into the next barber's shop he saw to rid his long hair of grease and his chin of tangled wiry follicles.

Finally, he strode out once more, feeling much more like himself after the makeover. His now bare face and conditioned hair attracted looks of deep yearning from women who passed him and envy from the men. Everyone who stepped close was almost shocked by the obvious beauty and symmetry of this man's face and the confidence that somehow shone through it.

The formerly dishevelled man was now a dapper gent but still one a little out of place in this city. In time gone by he had rarely had cause to visit Rome as it was the realm of his enemies and his younger and brasher counterpart. He was not convinced of his bearings in this unfamiliar landscape but he was sure it would not be difficult to find the seat of the catholic church even though some of the more venerable people inside may not welcome his return. He grinned as he looked forward to his imminent but unexpected and unwanted arrival.

II-XII – THE VATICAN CITY (SISTINE CHAPEL)

The owners of four sore heads sat silently on their mattresses as they attempted to regain their faculties. They had all slept deeply but no one felt refreshed as the slumber had been induced by sleeping gas and not by natural tiredness.

Instinctively the two girls reached for their compact mirrors, the distaste at the tired eyes that stared back at them clear to see. Dino was also keen to check his looks but did not want to undermine his masculinity by asking to borrow a looking glass.

The pounding in their heads was almost exactly like a hangover (although without the benefit of the fine wine and feelings of the previous day they all thought). The only plus side was that the headache and feeling of sickness did appear to already be dissipating and a few minutes later everyone was feeling almost human again when a rumbling sound of escalating volume heralded the return of the nun.

"Good morning everyone," the nun said cheerily as she walked in.

Luca narrowed his eyes as he responded sarcastically. "That is debatable. Are you not going to ask us if we slept well?"

Guiltily the nun looked down at the toes of her feet that protruded from underneath the bottom of her cassock. "There was no other way. I had to keep you here and this was the only way to make sure of that."

"In that case well done, you have succeeded," Dino added. "Now can you please let us out of here? You lured us down here with the promise of escaping and then you drug us!"

"It is not within my power to let you to leave. You will surely be killed trying or just hauled back inside again as I mentioned yesterday. The only possible way is with the help of what we keep in this room."

An emotional Laura now chipped in. "Look lady. You maybe a nun but you can still be prosecuted. If you don't let us go immediately I will ensure you are hauled through the courts as soon as we get out of here. I have some friends in some very high places you know!"

The nun looked to the ceiling. "So do I my dear but I am not sure even He can help us at the moment."

A resigned Alice, spoke for the first time that day. "Ok. Amuse us. Show us what dusty box can help us get out of here. Please."

"Very well," responded the nun. "But first I think it may help you to understand if you have a few words of instruction from our sponsor."

Before anyone could utter another word of incredulity, the nun turned to a large television placed on one of the shelves. Using the sleeve on her cassock, she wiped the dust from the screen and pressed a button on the DVD player sitting next to it. As the display eased into life the nun stepped back, bowed and crossed herself.

A crackling sound emanated from hidden speakers but no picture appeared until the word "Versace" leapt into view, the white text lurching in all directions and in and out of focus. The perplexed quartet looked on, beginning to wonder if for some reason they were being shown an advert by the famous designer.

A familiar voice then broke the monotony. *"How do you turn on this damned thing?"* said the now deceased ex-Pope from beyond the grave, the others gasping in surprise.

No further speech was offered as the "Versace" emblem shrunk from view as it was revealed to be printed on a pair of underpants sported by the pontiff, the waistband clearly visible on his retreating behind, the protective cassock beached high on his bent back. Without warning the former leader of the Catholic Church spun around to face the camera, still seemingly unaware it was already filming. Peering into the lens like an inquisitive animal inspecting a burrow, a single triumphant uttering was emitted and the camera shook as it was manhandled by an unseen hand. The screen went black, the camera now turned off. Seconds later and the image of the pope had returned, now sitting square in front of the camera, his cassock now fully unfurled and his sparse gray hair straightened.

126

Only a slight flush belied his recent exertions with 'modern technology' as he started to speak to his small audience in the confident, authoritative but kindly manner with which he had become famous before his untimely demise. *"Good day to you all. If you are now watching this video then it means I have almost certainly been imprisoned against my will, expelled from the Vatican by force or, most likely, I have been killed. The only plus side of such an unfortunate event is that I realized such plans were afoot and put certain steps in place to mediate the effects. Those steps involve you, you many hundreds of healthy young men and women were chosen especially for a trait you all share that will become important only later. For now training, knowledge and a fight awaits you but I have faith in you, my hundreds of warriors, faith that you can save the Vatican from the forces of tyranny!"*

The pope signed off with a flourish that was only slightly diminished when he stooped forward to turn off the camera, revealing a forest of silver chest hair as his loose garments billowed.

The nun looked anywhere but at the group, sheepishly avoiding any eye contact from the now petrified and frankly perplexed quartet.

"So where are these hundreds of which the dead Pope speaks?" Dino said in a raised voice. "Are they hiding somewhere in this great room ready to join us?"

The nun looked back awkwardly. "I think his holiness sadly expected many more to respond to his plea." Before anyone had a chance to berate her further, the cloaked woman turned back to the wall and flicked a bank of switches. Suddenly the visible universe as they knew it doubled in size as a ceiling light fluttered on in the distance. Another light even further away ignited into life, then another and another. In a few seconds, a dozen lights or more now illuminated a path into the distance showing the room to be many times vaster than they could ever have imagined. The group could not clearly make out the back wall, not because it was so far away but due to what now lay in between. Everyone else, apart from the nun, was mesmerized by what they saw in front of them.

The nun now walked into the newly revealed part of the chamber. "Very few people know this is all here and of course there is a very good reason for that. If anyone outside the Vatican knew of the existence of this place it would change the course of history…and probably mean the downfall of the Christian church. In fact even the Camerlengo doesn't know about this repository. He is already planning to sell off priceless treasures in the museums upstairs which will make him and his cronies all billionaires but if they found this place..."

"...They would be able to run the world," interrupted Dino robotically.

"Exactly", replied the nun. "What we have here is over five thousand years of artefacts that, officially, no longer exist. Everything you can see is laid out in chronological order, from the oldest, just up ahead, to the most recent against the farthest wall. Firstly, on our right, these weather-beaten planks of wood are our oldest relic although they only resurfaced in one of Saddam Hussein's private palaces during the last Gulf War. They may not look like much but they are the last remnants of Noah's Ark, protected from decay centuries ago by being preserved in a special embalming resin." The nun walked on a few steps. "Next on our right we have some old scrolls written in an ancient dialect of Aramaic that were clearly intended to form part of the Old Testament but were omitted for reasons lost in the mists of time. It took a team of scholars over a century to decipher the meaning and when they did, the result was so alarming, one of the experts died of shock on the spot."

"What do they say?" asked an inquisitive Alice.

"Oh it would not be wise for me to tell you much for a myriad of good reasons but one passage does refer to God being both man and woman and admitting monkeys were 'of the family of man'."

Suitably baffled the group followed the nun through the basement on a journey through time. "And here we have the writings of Jesus himself," continued the nun in awe, pointing towards an ancient looking book, protected within a glass case.

Dino scoffed. "That is nothing new! The writings of Jesus are inscribed in the bible."

"Oh yes, but not these writings. Remember the miracles he performed? Curing blindness at will, walking on water and turning water into wine? It is all explained in here by the man himself. For example, these open pages show exactly how he fed the multitudes with only five loaves and two fishes. It really is all just a matter of bending the laws of physics slightly with a little clever chemistry and a few willing minds.

Everyone crowded round with scepticism which they immediately shed as they began to follow the simple diagrams with their eyes. "Of course," said Dino. "It's all so simple when you see how it's done. A bit like a magic trick!"

"Indeed," replied the nun. "Although he did possess some powers that could not be explained though, even now. He truly was a unique individual."

Dino was keen to know more. "Why did he not share the knowledge of these powers with everyone?"

The nun shook her head sadly. "It has been noted in the scriptures that this was indeed the original wish but it was soon realized that there were too many people in the world who would have used these gifts for their own willing and not for the good of humankind, the same has never been truer than in these times of course. The human nature to control and have power over others is too strong in some to allow these learnings to be shared. Look at Communism for example. That should have worked but failed. There is always someone, at the very *least* one person, who is too tempted to abuse any power they have been given. Therefore the power and the knowledge housed here has been kept safe by the church and only lent out sparingly over the millennia when it was felt humanity needed a nudge in one direction or the other."

Laura continued her probing. "Who has been given these powers? I do not remember anyone else being able to turn water into wine! And who are you to say they should be housed here?"

"They are here because they have always been here. In the early days this place of God, this holy centre, was the only safe place of sanctuary that could protect such dangers. Over the proceeding centuries there have been many discussions about whether it all should remain here but where better to keep a secret than in the heart of the Catholic Church? As for who has been granted these powers…you would be surprised. Amazed in fact. Wherever there has been a pivotal moment in Western society over the last two millennia, chances are something from this space was given to the person or movement that initiated that change. Many sparks of imagination have been lit from here, hundreds of eureka moments originating not from grey matter but these dusty shelves. Of course most of the time these chosen few did not realize our influence and thought they had given birth to their own world-changing revelations. You may think you know how these thoughts and ideas are planted in fertile brains but it is not hypnosis or drugs or brain-washing but usually merely a suggestion placed from a friend, colleague or loved one. Often we have been even more subtle though. A passerby may have been wearing something that triggered an idea. Once even an apple falling out of a tree. You see we seek the people with the latent ability, the possibility for greatness and just give them that unseen little push out from behind the curtains and onto the bright lights of the stage. Nobody has turned water into wine since Jesus as that particular act has not been required since but other equally seemingly incredible feats have been achieved and not reported or, more likely, misreported over time."

A captivated Dino opened his mouth. "The falling apple was you? You mean Isaac Newton discovered gravity because of the Catholic Church?"

"Yes, he was one of many in a long list. It may seem odd that the church was helping a scientist but we knew the truth of the world and the universe, we always have. We always knew that to keep power and faith in the church we had to aid certain sharp minds to gradually alter the way people think about the physical world without a sudden rebellion against the apparent traditional views of the church. Others helped in a similar regard at different times. Some Roman emperors, Copernicus, several kings, renaissance leaders, even modern presidents…Sadly we did make one or two mistakes with our choices though."

"Copernicus was hated and prosecuted by the church though wasn't he?" said Luca.

"Outwardly yes, we had to keep up that pretence but a few chosen people knew he was being used as a rudder to steer society out of troubled waters".

130

Quietly Laura spoke again. "Can we go back to the beginning please. Who exactly *was* Jesus?"

The nun laughed loudly, surprising the others. "If only I knew. If only any of us knew. However, I suspect we are not meant to know. Is he the son of God? To be honest I am not sure myself. As a Christian I am meant to accept his existence without question but knowing what I know I cannot help but to wonder whether he is or was a human being like no other or…"

"Or…" Laura prompted impatiently. "…Was He a time traveller from a more advanced future or even an alien?" All I know is that He was not a mere man. He was not someone that was chosen, *He chose* to create the church. *He chose* to create us."

All were now stunned into silence again as Laura began to ponder further. Was it blasphemy to wonder what it would have been like to be with Jesus as His wife? Surely if she had been born at that time he would have represented the pinnacle of her ambitions in a man? He was someone who wielded ultimate power and adulation. She had always craved a man with fabulous amounts of money, grand houses and the fastest cars but someone with the powers he held at his magical healing fingertips and levitating heels would trump the attraction of the richest and most charismatic billionaire. In her head she thought of the painting of the Last Supper analyzed in recent films. What if the popular theorists were right? What if it wasn't John sitting to the right of Jesus but actually Mary Magdalene, A woman with equally lofty demands in her partner and a historic version of her very self!

If she could not have Jesus, the 2,000 year age gap and death being too big an obstacle perhaps, she thought, could she attain the next best thing? Maybe one of these secretly powerful men the nun referenced would sate her craving? She made a mental note to later quiz the nun on who had recently been touched with these powers. Perhaps a European president or king? Her heart raced at the thought of being at their side as they helped to gently nudge society onto the right course.

Alice was quiet but now not because she was overawed by the fantastic yarn she was being spun. She had stopped listening a while ago when talk of Jesus had reminded her of the *Immaculate Conception* and that in turn had reminded her of what currently rested in her bag and its consequences. Discreetly, so nobody else saw what she was doing, she prized the zip open, fumbling around in the miasma of its grubby interior before she found what she was looking for. She stared at the small pen-like device as if she could change the words printed on the display by concentrating hard enough. It was no use though, it still defiantly displayed *1-2 weeks pregnant* in bold black lettering. A swollen lump formed in her throat but as a wetness threatened to form around her eyes she suppressed it before anyone else noticed. She tried not to think about the events that had led to this but the thoughts and images would not go away, circling endlessly like the few remembered words of a song spinning around in your head when you are trying to sleep.

It had been yet another brief infatuation she had not wanted and had not asked for but somehow this latest man had gotten embedded deep under her skin like a tick. She smiled at the analogy, although it was an unfair one. In truth he had been more like an addictive drug that was difficult to obtain and the brief pleasure of the arrival only just worth the weeks of enforced abstinence, waiting for the next hit. If only, she thought, she had been able to wean herself off before she became dependant as she could not afford the high price of such dangerous substances as love.

Work always came first, as work led to recognition, to opportunities, to America, to stardom, to happiness. She did not have time for foolish affairs of the heart that distracted her from where her life must lead. Most of the time Alice was able to adhere strictly to this edict but, every so often, someone would get around her defences.

This time, the combatant that had broken down her barriers had met her on St. Patrick's day. Normally Alice was a light drinker but the carnival atmosphere of the day had massaged her strict resolutions into submission. This year the celebrations fell on a Friday, giving everyone even more of an excuse to start the weekend with a bang. She had been drinking outside her favourite Irish pub, laughing raucously with her friends and other acquaintances when she saw another friend weaving through the unstable crowd towards her.

She greeted her with a warm hug, alcohol increasing the length and force of the embrace. The friend introduced Alice to a young man she knew from Ireland, an old acquaintance she had met when they had studied together at university in Dublin. Alice actually vaguely remembered the man from a previous visit but then he had held no interest for her. Somehow today was different. Immediately he caught her attention with his height, his sturdy frame and his unusual locks of wavy flame-red hair. She feigned indifference to him but her friend smiled wanly, knowing Alice well enough to spot the telltale if subtle change in her body language.

For the next couple of hours they all drank and talked although Alice let the others do most of the talking, giving her time to take in the occasional sneaky glance of her new desire. After a while she learned his name was Rory and that he lived and worked and Dublin and played rugby at the weekends. That was pretty much all she could work out though as, for the benefit of Rory, the conversation was being carried out mainly in English. She knew a few words but certainly not enough to join in with a fluent conversation and she suspected his Italian was at much the same level. His accent was charming though, you did not need to understand the words to know that. She was not sure yet if he was single but that did not matter much at this point and it would be up to him to make any decisions of that nature anyway.

As a group they decided to move on to another bar across the city. It was too far to walk and Alice's friend went to get her car. (She had been drinking but not too much to drive of course, never too much). Alice had her moped so she casually offered Rory a ride in the best english she could muster. He looked surprised but he accepted, nimbly catching the helmet she suddenly hurled in his direction like a rugby ball. Alice hopped on the vespa gracefully but Rory looked at the small bike as a novice jockey might look at a fearsome horse. Eventually he placed himself directly behind her on the small second seat that made intimate body contact inevitable. As soon as he reached around to gently hold the sides of her slender body, Alice kicked the bike into life, the adrenaline from the touch of his hands making her turn the accelerator handle a little more than she had anticipated. Startled by the sudden movement, Rory tightened his grip and his inhibitions loosened. To Alice those hands were electrified, making her body tingle as they gently indented the space beneath her ribs.

After a few short minutes careering along slippery cobbled streets, they reached their destination. Alice turned off the engine, took off her helmet and shook her hair loose. She turned around to look at Rory and explained to him slowly in Italian that they needed to wait for her friends to find somewhere to park on the ever-crowded streets. She knew he would probably not understand the words but she thought he would perhaps grasp the meaning and indeed he nodded and seemed to understand. Her neck ached as she twisted back to look into his azure blue eyes. Words of any language were not required for them to both understand what they both wanted to do next as they synchronously leaned in to kiss each other on the lips, gently and respectively at first but then passionately, neither of them conscious of the small throng of drinkers standing outside the adjacent nightclub that began to snigger and whistle. Their lips eventually parted but their meeting left an invisible string between them that kept them closely connected for the rest of the evening. They danced, they kissed and they even managed to converse within the limits of the Alice's fractured English and the help of her friends who had all managed to muster a much better grasp of the guttural language. At the end of the evening Rory raised his eyebrows suggestively but she explained openly that she never slept with anyone on the first night. It was a rule she never broke. She knew she would not be able to resist the temptation for more than a day but that was not the point. In her head, not sleeping with someone when they first met was what separated her from common wanton women and upheld the value her mother had always instructed to place on herself.

Rory was only in Bologna for the next three days and in that short time their bond grew as they laughed and they played. She was smitten but as always, she refused to let it show too much. Fawning would never do, it was a weakness and she vowed never to be the victim by letting too much emotion rise to the surface. Besides, what good would ever come of it? Her destiny was in Milan, Rome and then America, not here and certainly not in Ireland. She chose not to see him the morning he went to the airport, deciding it would be easier for him that way. She tried not to think about what feelings he may have.

They kept in touch over the next few months. She laughed at his emails that were written in Italian using a cheap translation website and they shared the odd photo. It felt like a holiday romance that was going to fade out and she was happy with that. She had work to do and lived in another country for goodness sake. That all changed though when he visited again. It was nearly six months since they had first seen each other but that time apart evaporated like a summer morning mist as they continued seamlessly from where they had left off. They were now even able to communicate more easily as he had learned a little more of her mother tongue.

They acted like any other young couple in love (not that the emotive word itself had been uttered between them) until the day he had to leave again. They rode once more in tandem back to the train station on her Vespa. The once frightened jockey behind her was now a steady experienced rider, using his thighs to keep his balance more than his hands that still gripped Alice's waist. They walked together in silence through the grey ticket hall, through the huge doors and out onto the grey platform. Rory seemed to know that these would be the last moments they would be together in any sense other than friends. No words had been exchanged that even hinted at such a decision but they both knew they could not afford the high emotional and financial price that came with a long-distance relationship. As always she remained tight-lipped and poker-faced and could even still look him in the eyes even though she could feel a painful knot swelling in her throat. The train arrived and Rory reluctantly boarded. He rushed to find his seat and threw his bag down so he could look out the scratched window for one last vision of his Italian beauty. The weight of his heavy heart made it fall into the pit of his stomach as he vainly scanned the platform.

Alice had already left the station and left Rory behind her, physically and mentally. She wiped her mind clean of him in an instant and had not thought about him at all in the days that followed until now, as she stared again at the pregnancy indicator that refused to change its simple but life-changing missive.

Luca boyishly plunged his hands into his jacket pockets, subconsciously flipping the plastic discs his fingers found in each recess. He listened to the words the nun was saying but their meaning did not sink in. It was as if his brain had reached saturation point. The sponge was full of water and it could take on no more. Out of curiosity he retrieved the items from his pockets, not remembering what the plastic discs were that he fondled. Lifting up the small items he saw they were identical sturdy red and black discs emblazoned with a picture of a golden lion, rampant and rearing as if preparing to pounce. The lion was one of the symbols of Venice and these chips were clearly from its first and still most popular casino. He smiled sadly. This was the jacket he had worn at the casino last night when he had accompanied a very grateful and very bored wife back to her hotel apartment. He commonly received such trinkets from the ladies he entertained but normally they were thrust gratefully into his hand, like pocket money given to a small boy, instead of being secreted into the pockets of his clothing when he wasn't looking.

He thought he knew the value of the discs from the colour but turned them over anyway to see the other side. He nearly dropped each one in shock as he saw the figure printed in bold silver letters that were bent around the circumference of each chip. It was not the *"10 Euros"* he had been expecting but *"100,000 Euros"*! Each! The two small bits of plastic represented more money than he had made in the last five years put together, probably more. Instinctively he now coveted them more closely, pressing them deep into his closed fists before placing them safely in the very bottom of his bag when no one else was looking. He had often dreamed of what it would be like to have so much money but for some unknown reason he found he was not overwhelmed with immediate euphoria.

"And lastly we have the Renaissance period," said the nun, at last catching the attention of Alice and Luca as well as the rest of the group. It was clear they had both missed a few hundred years of history during their personal periods of reverie.

Dino walked over to a strange looking flying contraption nearby, talking as he touched one of the fabric wings. "This isn't possible," he directed back to the others. "These things were never made. They must be re-creations," he said dismissively to everyone and no one in particular.

The nun looked on proudly. "Not true. It is another well suppressed piece of history that everything this person drew, he also created."

Laura had to be sure. "By this person you mean…"

"Yes," the nun pre-empted. "This is one of the unknown works of *Master di Leonardo de ser Piero*, more commonly known as *Leonardo da Vinci*."

II-XIII – THE VATICAN (INSIDE AND OUT)

The now well-dressed man turned heads as he strode confidently on the relatively short walk towards the river Tiber that separated Rome from the Vatican on the opposite bank. Presently the man arrived at one of the bridges that spanned the dirty waters below, although he would not be able to cross. A barricade of tanks and barbed wire were placed in his path whereas below gunboats patrolled the river itself. Shielding his eyes from the sun, he looked across the river and towards the holy city. In front of the mighty walls was now a 'no-man's-land', a clear band of tarmac left vacant by the visible encircling Italian army to avoid potential provocation from the forces within.

The man smiled, reflecting how little changed despite hundreds of years of history passing like so much water under the bridge in front of him. Ignoring the barricades he quickly descended a flight of steps cut out of the stone embankment that led to the water's edge below. On the shore of the wide river he paused only briefly before carrying on down the steps as they sunk into the water. Unconcerned by the rising water around him he continued until completely submerged and when the steps ended he drifted down to the riverbed. Two minutes later the figure emerged dry on the opposite bank, unnoticed by all the patrolling forces. Calmly he ascended the steps that mirrored those on the opposite bank, disappearing into the vacated streets, heading straight for St. Peter's square in the heart of the Vatican.

"I told you not to touch that!" The frustrated nun scolded Dino like a mother would her child.

"How could I not?" he responded. "This place is like a toy shop crossed with a military museum!" Dino grinned as he reluctantly vacated the seat of Leonardo's flying contraption that looked like a primitive helicopter with an open cockpit and blades that were wide and delicately curved like a pair of twisted sycamore seeds. At first the controls of the machine had been perplexing but, with a little trial and error of pulling at levers and peddling furiously with his feet, he had been able to hover the ancient contraption a few inches off the ground if only for a couple of seconds at a time.

The nun was relieved when he finally disembarked, his short attention span now held by another one of Leonardo's secret inventions, a strange tank that looked more like a giant dumpling.

The nun reflected that she had been surprised by the lack of shock from the others when she had declared to them that Leonardo da Vinci was the creator of all these priceless works. Perhaps modern films were to blame? The young adults of today were all too used to special effects and outlandish tales. They probably thought this was still all an elaborate hoax and she was not telling the truth. This was an issue as she would need them all to believe everything in time. With a sigh she bent down at the floor, tracing an invisible symbol on the unmarked surface.

In moments, the building shook before a huge portion of the floor they were all standing on began to rise. The four young Italians and the nun were lifted steadily upwards but this time they were not alone. With them on the platform were all of Leonardo's creations, neatly assembled in regimented rows as if ready for battle. Along with the helicopter and the dumpling tank there was some sort of glider, several immense catapults and a couple of common trebuchets. Only Luca dared to peer over the edge of the unfenced plate that had risen too quickly for any of them to think of jumping off. He alone was rewarded with a view of the entire basement from some thirty meters high. From that elevated viewpoint he could just make out what appeared to be the perimeter walls that he estimated to be at least a mile distant in each direction.

As Luca looked down the others preferred to look up as they approached the solid inevitability of the concrete ceiling. As they neared the looming construction, they instinctively crouched and cowered but then a long vertical line of light appeared above them that gradually broadened. In a few short seconds they could see the light was sunlight and the widening line revealed the sky. The aperture was soon thankfully broad enough to allow the whole platform to pass through.

Up and into the blinding light they went, waiting as one to see what peril would now face them. Fear spread through them, especially Laura who reached out for Dino's hand to clasp. He responded with a weak smile, trying to show bravado that he did not at that moment possess.

In St. Peter's square, the Camerlengo addressed his troops as they lined up in front of him on the sun-baked piazza. "Gentlemen, we are approaching our finest hour. With your help all the ancient artefacts within the Vatican Museums have been catalogued and they are ready to be shipped out to the discrete customers we have identified around the world. We have a especially commissioned train waiting at the Vatican's very own railway station within the grounds. Once my lackeys have finished loading the priceless goods, the train will depart from here to Italy and from there each item will be delivered by air and sea to its new home. Never again will the church have such wealth and power. It will be shared amongst the many individuals around the world. In addition, as I have said, you will all share in a part of this wealth. I will make you all millionaires, if that is what you choose to be of course. This, my friends, is the very start of a re-distribution of the gross and unnecessary assets that the catholic church has built up over the centuries. This next act will bring the church to its knees and then the final curtain call we are planning will kill them off for good!"

Many of the soldiers laughed, revelling in the secret they all knew about the new pontiff that would send shockwaves through the world.

The Camerlengo continued. "Wealth and victory will need to be earned though. Soon, you will all prove you are not merely ceremonial soldiers gaily dressed in garish pantaloons but true harbingers of war. You will have your first and only battle that will ultimately be a glorious one. Your names will go down in the history of the Swiss Guards as the only ones worthy of the name as you will actually be guarding the new Pope of the common people here on his land, on the battlefield we will create.

"The world of today is one in turmoil as we have created an event nobody expected or ever dared to plan for. They do not attack us

140

because we are in an independent state and we have not contravened any international laws. Nevertheless, rest assured my soldiers, they will re-write the statute books and create new laws and regulations to ensure we have fallen foul of them. Then they will attack and we must defend this place in the name of Switzerland!" Punching the air he urged his foot soldiers to follow. Obediently they copied him, hailing a blood-curdling war cry in return.

What fools they were, thought the Camerlengo and how easy they were to manipulate! It had been so simple to tap into their latent desire to be warhorses and not the show ponies they had been. He would not join them in battle though. He knew he would be long gone and safely on the Vatican train well before the first drop of blood hit these famous cobbles. He did not care how well they fought as long as they put up enough of a distraction to allow him and his precious cargo to speed out of here on the Pope's own carefully protected single-track railway line. The guards had no hope in defending this tiny principality against the forces of the modern world and would never see the riches they thought would follow.

The plan was almost set but one possible fly in the ointment remained in the form of an old rival from Milan who had initially instructed him to carry out this audacious scheme on his behalf in return for a share of the spoils. The Camerlengo had agreed to the plan but then double-crossed his partner in crime, reducing him to a fraction of his former size and imprisoning him in a place from which he knew escape would be improbably if sadly not impossible.

Concentrating again on matters at hand, the Camerlengo focused on his troops once more, preparing himself for one last battle cry before he made his hasty escape but for some reason they had all turned away from him. He was ready to admonish their collective lack of concentration and respect before he saw what they were looking at as his body of soldiers parted neatly in two like the Red sea being commanded by Moses. All his troops on the far side of the split leapt the widening gulf to join their comrades before the thin veneer of the famous cobbled circular courtyard peeled back as if it was the opening eye of a giant.

III

III-I – THE VATICAN CITY (ST PETER'S SQUARE)

The four reluctant saviours shielded their eyes from the increasing intensity of light as they rose through the ceiling with the nun and into the great courtyard outside St. Peter's church. Their eyes adjusted and they felt exposed, almost naked as they were viewed upon by hundreds of eyes owned by the Swiss Guards. Standing in the midst of such a crowd was a strange experience after the gloomy isolation to which they had so quickly become accustomed. The only compensation was that the lines of soldiers looked as bewildered as they did.

As the platform stopped, forming a new smooth circular floor in the middle of the cobbles, the quartet resisted their initial instincts to run towards the road that ran past the side of the square, understandably hesitant at the sight of the gun-wielding armed forces. But move they did as the great platform on which they were standing divided in the middle to form a great chasm that extended across the entire the piazza. For reasons they did not know, they opted to leap with the nun to where the Swiss Guards stood instead of the opposing side of the ravine that bordered Rome and freedom.

Regaining his composure after the shocking and rather dramatic arrival and the carving of the ground by his feet, the Camerlengo addressed the new attendees. "I am not going to begin to understand how you escaped from the chapel but it matters not now as I have everything in place. Please feel free to leave if you wish. I will not try to stop you. Go back to your little lives in Italy. Mind you, I do not fancy your chances out there beyond the Vatican walls. Anyone trying to leave at this time will surely be shot by the Italian army unless of course they have gorged themselves on their wine-fuelled five course lunch!" The Camerlengo laughed, his chuckling echoed by some of the Swiss guards, possibly now out of a certain unease as opposed to a show of appreciation of his xenophobic humour. "I can give you a choice however. You can choose to stay on our side, soon to be the victorious side I may add. You can share in the spoils of war, which I can assure you will be great, or you can wave the white flag and be rescued when the outside forces storm this place. You may have a tough job in convincing them that you are not in league with me though before they open fire on you all."

"We could always fight against you!" said Dino bravely, tapping Leonardo da Vinci's tank with the palm of his hand admiringly.

"With those toys you have dug up from the basements? Don't make me laugh. They were always Leonardo's fanciful dreams that should have stayed on parchment or even better in his wine-soaked head. You are more likely to blow yourselves up than cause the slightest harm to me or my troops! I bet you haven't even worked out how they operate, have you?"

His bluff called, Dino looked crestfallen and the others looked on with increased concern.

"Yes, but *I* know how they work," said a new booming and seemingly bodiless voice.

The Camerlengo's face drained of colour. He knew that voice but it could not be *him*, surely there was no possible way he could be *here*!

"I know what you are thinking Camerlengo," the voice called, seemingly close but somehow from all directions at once, the sound reverberating around the arc of pillars that rimmed the square. "How could I be here, so far from where you left me alone, stricken, small and weak?" The Camerlengo spun around. The voice almost seemed to be at his back now but nobody was there. The guards were all spooked, the chattering sound of their guns shaking as the brainwashed but novice battalion feared the unknown.

"Show yourself, you cretin!" the Camerlengo shouted, his confidence now only maintained by a pistol he produced from underneath his flowing cloak.

"Gladly," responded the mysterious newcomer as he emerged from amongst the closely-knit bodies of the Swiss Guards behind the Camerlengo. The Camerlengo turned to face his foe but before he could point his gun it had already been deftly taken from him, the well dressed man hurling it far out into the square where it bounced harmlessly on the cobbles.

144

"You old fool. Do you really think you can stop me by taking my gun when I have a small army at my disposal?" the Camerlengo said as beamed patronizingly at the other man.

"What is an army without weapons though my young pretender?"

The Camerlengo was perplexed by the comment until he saw that to a man his guards had all dropped their weapons on the ground in front of them. The Camerlengo dropped to his knees in supplication. "Please forgive me Leo. I always intended to rescue you from your prison and return you to your full height but there was not time before the outside world put me under siege."

"What rubbish you speak, but no matter. You will pay later for your treachery but in the mean time I have some unfinished business to attend to." Stepping away from the Camerlengo he spied the incongruous grouping of young adults and the nun. "Ah, *what* and perhaps, of more import, *whom* do we have here? One of you I recognize but not the others."

The nun stepped forward to address the stranger, placing herself between him and the four young adults behind her, a pawn on a chessboard protecting the more valuable pieces. "So, you have somehow returned," she said with some disdain.

"Yes, I am back here in the deep south, no thanks to you my dear lady." Now theatrically stepping to one side he looked beyond the nun to speak to the others directly. "Please excuse me for my rudeness at not addressing you earlier my guests. My name is Leonardo da Vinci and it appears as though I need to congratulate you for freeing my instruments of war that have been so rudely sequestered for so long by this evil woman and her kind."

The nun scowled. "It is *you* who is the evil one Leonardo. An evil man with great talents that should have been put to such better use," the nun shouted in his direction.

"*Better use.* What an interesting choice of words sister. Many would say that the pursuit of science and *not* the church really *is* "better use" but then we have had this discussion more than once over time and I think we will always agree to disagree on this matter."

"Disagree we always have but no longer my little artisan. You may have escaped twice but there will be no third resurrection."

"Oh don't bore me, I do hate such serious talk from a lady, especially one of your pedigree Joan. Listen, I have a deal for you. It appears that as I have been double-crossed by our pontiff's assistant here, the dear Camerlengo, we therefore both now have a common foe and you can help me to get something I want in return for vanquishing this ancient fiend."

"Okay. Humour me Leonardo. What is in you want from me?"

Leonardo paused dramatically before responding. "What have I always wanted my dear? What one thing have I strived to succeed in over all these centuries?"

The nun shook her head fiercely. "No. You will never have *that*. You know it will be the end of the Catholic Church if that happens, probably even Christianity."

"I don't think so Joan. You and the church just need to adapt to a different way of thinking. Call it modernization if you will. Everything else has had to do it over time to survive so why should the church be exempt? It is merely natural evolution. Besides, what choice do you have? I could walk away but, If I do, our foe will succeed in stripping the Vatican of its assets and history. The empty buildings will then probably be damaged or even destroyed by the over-zealous western forces champing at the bit to fire off a few missiles. What then my saintly friend? What would the Catholic Church be without the Vatican? It would be like Islam without Mecca, Paris without the Eiffel Tower, Scientology without Tom Cruise."

The nun paced up and down for a few seconds before finally coming to a decision. "Alright," she said meekly. "I think we can come to some sort of compromise. Let's just rid ourselves of Michelangelo first."

Leonardo clapped his hands together. "Excellent! I knew you'd see my way of thinking eventually. It's just a shame it took you so long! Now, who are these creatures you have behind you, placing their grubby mitts all over my works of genius?"

146

"These *creatures* as you call them are the late Pope's picks for this generation. One of them will be the chosen one, the next saviour of the church."

Leonardo thought for a moment. "Of course, we are at the peak of the cycle once more. Twenty-three years have passed since the last alignment, although that was of course a bit of an anti-climax."

"At least we stopped you in '58," the nun said defensively."

Leonardo barely heard the response from the nun, now visibly distracted by something or, more accurately, by some*one*. Transfixed, he moved stealthily towards the object of his undivided attention, the refined Laura. Cautiously he stepped towards her as if she was a timid woodland creature that might be scared away by too sudden a movement. Now within reach of his quarry he outstretched a half open hand that reached forward to gently cup the face of the young maiden under her small chin. If any other man had approached and touched her in such a way, Laura would have slapped his hand away but somehow she was immediately captivated by this man who was devastatingly handsome at close quarters.

Leonardo finally found his voice once more. "My dear flower. In all my considerable years I have rarely seen a face of such unrivalled beauty, especially in a woman."

Laura blushed uncontrollably.

"I have no doubt your proportions adhere strictly to the golden ratio, probably to many decimal points! Have you heard of the fabled golden ratio?"

Laura shook her head slowly, already falling for the deep timbre of his voice and flattered by his obvious adoration.

Leonardo removed his hand and stepped back as if giving himself space to perform. "The golden ratio is the most beautiful form in nature, expressed in the language of mathematics. It is something that can be found in the arrangement of branches in the trees along the stems of plants and in the veins of their leaves. It is even seen embedded in the skeletons of animals and the geometry of growing crystals. I think the great mathematician Adolf Zeising described it best when he said it was a universal law that contains the ground-principle of all forms striving for beauty and completeness in the realms of both nature and art. It is something that permeates as a paramount spiritual ideal, all structures, forms and proportions, whether cosmic or individual, organic or inorganic, acoustic or optical. But Zeising went on to say that it finds its fullest realization in the human form. In layman's terms he was referring to the ratio of the length of your proportions being 1.618 times their widths, a relation which I am convinced proliferates in your stunning face…and no doubt elsewhere."

Leonardo reached out once more and began to trace a line down the side of Laura's face from the top of her head to the base of her jaw. Laura felt the touch as electricity passing through her.

"For example, the length *here*…" he whispered, "will be 1.618 times the width *here*" he continued as his finger turned through 90 degrees, ending at the tip of her chin.

"With such incredible features I have a very strong urge to paint you," he said with eulogy.

"And I have a strong urge to hit you!" responded a shunned Dino, feeling suddenly displaced in his position as alpha male and suitor to the woman with the golden ratios between them. Dino strode towards the man who called himself Leonardo, not afraid to confront the supposed Renaissance artisan as to what this charlatan would say or do next. He only just resisted the temptation to strike him, his curiosity only just the victor as the more powerful emotion. "Who are you *really*, apart from same crazy person who thinks he is a long dead artist and inventor. And what does all this posturing and talk of chosen ones and past battles have to do with us?"

Leonardo turned to Dino. "If you are patient, which I know must be difficult for someone of such base emotions, then I will elucidate. Obviously my old prodigy the Camerlengo and the lady of the cloth here have failed to give you the courtesy of a full explanation. After all, I am sure the Camerlengo, the man *I* know as Michelangelo can wait for me to finish." He turned around to view the younger man and his army but the forces had slunk off unnoticed! "Ah, it appears your friends have gone off to play hide and seek!"

The stunned Camerlengo feverishly looked one way and the next but his troops were nowhere to be seen, either having scarpered silently by their own volition or spirited away by one of Leonardo's parlour tricks. Furious but with no immediate course of action that sprang to mind he glowered at the old master before slinking away to find them.

"Anyway where was I?" Leonardo continued. "Of course, I was about to give these young guns a little secret history lesson." He held his arms aloft where billowing clouds of vapour began to form above his head, widening and thickening until they coalesced into a slate grey screen that floated in the air. He lowered his arms and an image began to appear on the foggy screen, blurred at first but soon crystallizing, like a camera lens focusing until a sharp image of a verdant pasture could be clearly seen. Leonardo addressed the baffled group once more. "A battle has raged constantly for millennia right under the eyes of normal men and women. Only a few have been privileged to witness it and fewer still have taken part but those that have been involved benefited in the most sensational of ways. I am one of those lucky few.

"This war of which I speak began almost as soon as man could think beyond the capabilities of animals, when humans gained cognition of what they were and who they were. I think therefore I am, I am therefore I fight for my life, for my family, for my kin and for my genes that will be passed on. We possess the basic raw animal aggression to defend our genetic material and ourselves at all costs. Combined with the intellect that first burgeoned in early man, this created a formidable weapon indeed. But this weapon of intelligence is so deadly and its power so troubling to us that it gave birth to religion.

"From that first moment, the birth of the first religion, our lives were not truly our own and we began to depart from nature. With collective belief there was power and religion grew with that power. In many cultures its growth was benevolent but in the west Christianity grew like a cancer, poisoning the host but growing within them largely unnoticed but often producing a dark venomous bile. Although, with every *yin* there is always a *yang*. The counteracting force to religion is science. Nature. The earth. Call it *Gaia* if you will.

And so, at almost exactly the same time as religion was created, so were the sciences. Of course it all started by accident. Someone would realize what conditions made a certain crop plant grow well, another found their ailment was helped by rubbing a certain leaf on their affected parts, someone discovered cooking meat on a fire made it taste better or easier to eat and so on. This knowledge was passed on and built on and improved. Using plants for healing became the foundations of medicine, the discovery of fire lead to physics and chemistry. The selective growing of crops was the building blocks of biology."

"The wealth of knowledge in the fields of nature and religion has grown exponentially over the last few thousand years alongside the seemingly steadying hand of religion but the two trains of thought have never seen eye to eye and one has always tried to dominate the other as the one true ideal path for humanity. This battle has raged openly and secretly for countless generations, one side winning a skirmish only for the other side to land a counter-blow. Innumerable papers, books and speeches have been written and delivered to try to convince people of the importance of science against religion but, despite falling congregations, the power of the church has prevailed and does so to this day."

"There have been pivotal moments over time though. One of the most critical of course being some two thousand years ago. Then the dominant religion in the civilized world at the seat of power was Judaism. Then Jesus arrived as the proclaimed saviour of man and a whole new religion, Christianity, was latterly born. You might think that was a battle between two factions of religion with science floundering unnoticed in the background but you would be very wrong my friends. You see the birth of Christianity was so nearly a comprehensive victory for science and nature.

"Jesus was not a religious man, it was the religion that was built around him and at a much later date when he was long gone. He was an egotist, a genius but most importantly and fundamentally a *scientist*. He built up a following, showing people how they should believe in science and not the god or gods they followed. He gave demonstrations of scientific knowledge by turning water into wine using advanced fermentation techniques, showed new recipes

150

allowing food to go further in times of famine and introduced new medicines that people used for healing. These were all things we use today but in those times they were seen as miracles. These endeavours were all written in the bible obviously, although the tales have been altered greatly by the religious scholars that scribed the bible so many years later, twisting the accounts of his demonstrations to suit their own religious aims. At the time Jesus thought he was finally winning the battle for science and nature but he had enemies he had greatly under-estimated. He knew the Jews wanted him out of the way as his new scientific ways were a threat to their religion but he also knew they were not the ruling power and they could not force his expulsion or death. It was the Romans who were in charge and he had not expected them to help out the Jews. And thus Jesus' scientific vanguard backfired in the most spectacular way as he was killed before he could engender the belief of science into the population. After a fallow period the religious powers at the time turned the strength of His legends to their advantage. And so a new religion was created around Him that burgeoned into a behemoth now followed by billions."

"However Jesus was not the only ambassador for science and in fact over the millennia there have now been hundreds who have tried at regular intervals in time, each one born 23 years from the last. In the same year, a similar messenger for religion is also brought into the world. Nobody knows why the births follow this period but the pattern never falters. Each 23 years, a new chosen one from each side of the great divide is born to join us others who are already here, as none of us chosen ones can ever truly die except under specific circumstances. It is true that at first we grow up in blissful ignorance like the mortals that surround us, even if some of us have a suspicion that we are somehow different. We are left to tread our own paths until we reach the critical age of 23 years. At that age, when we are barely adults, we are approached and made aware of who we are and the importance of our role. It is then we meet others at the time of the great gathering that occurs every 23 years. Often a great battle wages for that year. Sometimes it is not fought with the sword but with the pen, one side trying to win the eternal war with literal evidence rather than physical force but more often, like this year, weapons will be employed.

"My story is that I was lucky enough to be born in the Renaissance period in the heart of Tuscany where I was able to exert the talents I had been given to progress the cause of science. After my 23rd birthday people who realized I was a science emissary approached me. They tried to propel my ideas ready for the next peak in the 23-year cycle. In 1498, when I was 46, I painted *The Last Supper* as a message, a call to arms for the forces of nature and one in the eye for religion. Incidentally, 46 years of age is the point all missionaries stop growing any older, forever frozen in time at that middle age. For some of the more famous emissaries over time it has caused them issues to make themselves look older and then eventually faking their own deaths when the time suits them but you would be surprised how easy it is to trick people when they cannot conceive the truth.

"By the time I stopped growing old I had already built the weapons of war you see behind you. I attempted to use them in anger back then with many friends at my heel, storming south from Milan to here at The Vatican but we were never able to march on Rome. At that time the forces of the church were too strong. I was not sure who my counterpart was at that time, the church emissary of my same age, but he must have been there somewhere, pulling strings behind the scenes to thwart me and ensure any movement against the church would mean my certain incarceration. Still, I knew I would get another chance one day at one of the following meetings, each nearly a quarter of a century apart. I didn't think I would have to wait so long for my turn again though! What fools have tried and failed in the interim!

"Anyway, back to the present day. Obviously now you know I am an emissary and that our foe the Camerlengo is actually Michelangelo, a man who was originally 23 years my junior. In his first life he was certainly on the side of the church but I fear he is only on the side of himself nowadays, frankly an even more dangerous prospect. There is one more of our kind amongst us though and her devotion to the cause can surely not be questioned, despite being tried for heresy. Are you still seeing visions Joan? Or should I call you *Saint* Joan of Arc?"

The nun narrowed her eyes at the flamboyant fop. "Yes I am Joan or *Jeanne* as I was called back in those days. I was indeed burned at the stake by the church but I know that was the decision of evil bishops motivated by power and political gain. I know that God never doubted me. He wanted me as his warrior which was why, when people thought they were laying my charred body to rest I later rose again like yourself."

Leonardo shook his head in mock sadness. "Oh Joan, in that short statement you prove my way of thinking. 'Evil bishops motivated by power and political gain' you said. Can't you see your beloved church is rotten to the core and needs to be destroyed once and for all?"

"No. Never! There are always a few bad apples in the orchard but the church is a force for good and always will be!" said the former peasant heroine.

Smiling wanly Leonardo continued. "Well I would love to stand here and continue this discussion but sadly I think we now all have more pressing matters!" Dramatically the Renaissance man pointed towards the exit to the great square where a line of modern grey tanks trundled into the open space, their caterpillar tracks struggling to gain purchase on the smooth stones as a deep rumbling roar caused by the movement of their great combined mass thundered towards them.

Joan refused to look. "Which side are you even on Leonardo? You proclaim to be on the side of science but you want to help me stop Michelangelo destroying the Vatican, the home of the church?"

Leonardo laughed. "My choice is clear my saintly friend. Michelangelo has wronged me and I will vanquish him to ensure he does not leave here with all the Vatican's worldly assets. That is the first and foremost thought in my mind. That may mean by stopping him I assist you but be assured that will purely be by accident. I will fight these grey forces that have amassed here to oppose him but only because I want to combat him myself and I don't believe these Italian forces will let me join them. Now, if you will excuse me everyone I have some friends I must greet who are about to arrive to provide assistance. As for you lot, why not stay to see the show!"

Joan scowled and turned to the four bewildered visitors. "Quick my children. We must protect ourselves from these outside forces. I suspect Michelangelo has gone off to breathe some confidence into his troops and if he manages that we do not want to be caught in the cross-fire!"

Joan had barely finished speaking when her point was illustrated by the popping sound of gunfire that emanated from somewhere in the museums behind them, the bullets audibly whistling over their heads before creating sparks as they were harmlessly rebounded by the armoured tanks. "Follow me," she urged. "We can hide in the rooms behind the great pillars. We can be safe there and wait out this storm and who knows, maybe these soldiers will do us a favour and rid us of Michelangelo and Leonardo in one fell swoop!" Fearing for their lives, the four hostages dutifully followed Joan towards the safety of the Vatican buildings.

In St. Peter's square Leonardo watched the retreating huddle contemptuously with his hands on his hips. "You cowards! Do you really think that Michelangelo will be vanquished this easily? We have spent decades planning this very day, accounting for every eventuality. This little shower of bullets is a distraction whilst he smuggles the last of the valuables out from underneath everybody's noses! The only thing we can do is to go in after him using my weapons once I swiftly dispose of these modern irritants!"

Joan shouted back as she retired. "Your flimsy toys are only made of wood and leather, how are they going to last against modern weapons?"

"You think I did not think of that when I made them? You forget the powers I have over the natural elements my dear. With the power of my mind I have made the wood within them as strong as the best forged steel but as flexible as fresh rubber. Besides, I have other tricks up my sleeve and here are my friends to assist me."

From behind pillars to the side of the great piazza some figures emerged, unrecognizable at first but as they each walked confidently to the centre of the square, being tracked by the whirring gun turrets of the Italian tanks as they strode, their famous features became shockingly familiar to all. Isaac Newton was the first to shake the hand of Leonardo before the well-dressed and neatly coiffured man produced four apples from his pockets. He turned to face the tanks and juggled the red orbs with menace and intent. Next to arrive was

154

an unkempt man with tangled grey locks and a fine moustache. It was no less than Albert Einstein who nodded at the pair before pinching a large piece of chalk from behind his ear and using the writing implement to draw a line in front of them, followed by a drawing of a firing trebuchet and a lengthy equation. Last to arrive was a man in a long flowing cloak and beard. It was Archimedes who carried a musical triangle and a small set of hinged mirrors, the latter being his famous heat ray that caused the destruction of many an enemy ship in his original lifetime.

Leonardo stretched out his hands in the direction of the tanks that stood quiet still many metres away. With no warning, immediately in front of the nearest tank, the void between the opposing forces filled with water that welled up with speed from the hidden depths. The resultant canal was wider than the width that the tanks could bridge with their caterpillar treads, thus ensuring the metal beasts kept their distance.

"Just a little trick I learned from an old guy called Moses," Leonardo explained. "Now my ancient chums, let us ride my carriages to defeat these careless invaders who will have to be quashed before they reach Michelangelo! But, just before we do, I think someone else might be coming to our aid." He turned back once more to Joan and the four others, just before they disappeared into the Vatican's bowels, his eyebrows raised inquisitively.

Joan scoffed at his offer. "I cannot trust you and I am sure neither can anyone else here. We will end this madness without the help of you or your fanciful machines that never worked properly and your feeble powers that can move nature but not the will of man."

"Suit yourself Frenchy," Leonardo said mockingly. "I thought one of your number might join me though?" he continued, looking suggestively at Laura.

Laura stared at the man who had so desired her perfectly proportioned physical form and, inexplicably, she found herself moving from the safety of the colonnade, running towards Leonardo who embraced her with warmth and masculine rigidity.

"Laura! No!" shouted Dino in vain. He ran after her but had to almost immediately find cover as a hail of bullets ricocheted off the cobbles in front of him. With reluctance he allowed himself to be hauled back just as the battle commenced, the Italian tanks honing their guns on the ancient figures, Laura and their wooden toys. Leonardo took the arm of Laura, now his love struck companion and together they took a seat in one of his military contraptions.

The ancient scientific warriors took aim first. As Newton loaded his apples into the trebuchet honed with mathematical precision by Einstein, Leonardo fired arrows from his little wooden tank. Archimedes' ploy was to coax the enemy from their tanks that he achieved with his heat ray, focusing and intensifying the power of the overhead sun on the conductive metal machines of war until they changed colour from grey to red-hot. Hastily emerging from their scorching ovens the Italian soldiers were then aurally assaulted by the sheer volume and pitch of Archimedes' deafening musical triangle. The accurately aimed apples fired at gravity defying angles by Newton floored the few militiamen that had not succumb to the din, their hands firmly clasped over their bleeding ears.

III-II – THE VATICAN TO THE PAPAL VILLA

Michelangelo, the Camerlengo, was more than happy to appear the coward as he ran from his current foe and former friend. He saw nothing to gain and everything to lose from an exchange with Leonardo, be it verbal or physical. Besides time was not on his side if he wanted to escape and ensure the wealth of the Vatican museums joined him before he moved everything on to his secret bidders. Despite attracting the Italian army earlier than he anticipated and incurring the wrath of the Renaissance painter, he was still confident of success. He only wished he could have trusted someone more intelligent than his two bumbling assistants to oversee the transfer of goods. He had to admit though that for once, despite their calamitous tendencies, the dumb duo had done well. As the tottering twosome lifted the last of the heavy crates onto the train at the Vatican's very own railway station, Michelangelo ticked the last box on the very long order sheet and climbed on board, making the final preparations for the engine and its twenty three fully laden carriages to depart.

Half a mile away, in another part of the tiny principality, the sense of urgency that Joan was trying to instil in the others was being lost on one of the small group. The Venetian Luca had gradually fallen behind the others who were being urged to rush away from the booming sounds of war emanating from the square behind them. He was lost in his own world, staring once more at the valuable casino chips in his possession. He knew he should be delighted at this massive windfall that would mean he would be financially comfortable for the rest of his life. But he was surprised how much it had sickened him. Was it the feeling of being little more than a male prostitute knowing that he had received it from the aging woman he had entertained a couple of nights ago? Or was it because he knew she was so rich that even that fantastic sum would not be missed by her (or more importantly he guessed) her husband. Had she left the chip for him as a heart-felt bestowment that would enable him to change his life forever or as a condescending gesture of her power over him and everyone she felt was beneath her? Money was never a driver for Luca, he had seen through others it by no means guaranteed happiness and he proved this to himself one more time, feeling nothing when he snapped the almost priceless chips in two with his bare hands, the worthless halves discarded to the floor.

It was companionship and ultimately love that propelled him through life, the hope of finding that special person that made him get out of bed each morning when he felt those all too common low moments. And the first sparks of a new desire were ignited the first moment he spied Laura but the all too familiar story of 'natural selection' played out again as Dino took the initiative as an alpha male filling the space and time between himself and the quarry like an animal staking his claim on the female on heat. The only bittersweet moment to this all-too-familiar scenario was when Dino, the alpha male, was himself usurped by the flashy and daring Leonardo.

For Luca, confirmation of his familiar lowly place in this new pecking order was the final straw. Earlier the prospect of a new life born out of a TV show in the Vatican had given him hope. It had been a drug that had given him a brief high but now he was experiencing the crash the other side as the show had proved to be a sham. Luca was now a water-loving Venetian trapped in a tiny land-locked country embroiled in a bizarre war. He reasoned there was only one option now left open to him. Discretely he turned away from the others and snuck back towards the open square, the rumbling sounds of war increasing in volume and intensity as he strode towards the maelstrom. Out in the open again he weaved past Leonardo's ancient tank that was sliding nimbly over the cobbles and then he zigzagged with speed to evade the firepower of the modern tanks who fired mortars in return.

Luca ran towards the canal that divided the opposing forces, leapt into the waters and swam with purpose to the other side before heaving himself out to face the Italian tanks and infantry positioned at their rear. At first, the soldiers were perplexed, even scared and unsure what to do with a supposedly unarmed man pelting towards them but in the end their training took over as they aimed their guns, shouting at him to stop. But the man did not stop, he carried on running and so he became a threat to their self-preservation and the guns fired. Bullets from several pistols and rifles struck his body, his limbs flailing back with the impact, his legs first stumbling and then tripping him up. His stricken body was thrown to the cobbles where it continued to twitch under the continuing onslaught, blood now emerging from underneath his body, the thick red liquid oozing between the square flagstones.

Alice was alarmed when she felt a strange sensation in her belly. It felt like something had kicked her lightly from the inside but she knew this was impossible. She knew she was only one week pregnant, possibly two at the most and that the growing life inside her was barely larger than a pea. She looked down at her abdomen, stroking her stomach over her lightweight t-shirt. For years she had been careful to maintain a flat stomach, sometimes even concave or slightly toned but now she could definitely feel a gentle bump filling the space between the base of her rib cage and the top of her pelvic bone. Beads of cold sweat began to swell on her forehead as her brain struggled to come to terms with what appeared to be happening to her body. She was going through pregnancy, just as millions of women had done so before her but in Alice's case the incubation of her unborn child seemed to be occurring at a quite impossible rate!

Michelangelo ticked the last box on the last page of his hastily constricted delivery list of pilfered priceless artefacts from the Vatican museums. Wanting to waste no more time he was just about to hop into the engine car at the front of the train when, from behind him, the voice of a familiar figure stopped him in his tracks.

"Stop right there Michelangelo" said the diminutive form of Joan, flanked by Alice and Dino on either side.

Michelangelo did not turn around when he responded. "Why in the name of all that is holy should I bother?" he shouted as he pulled himself up onto the steps just as the train began to edge away from the tiny station. Due to its heavy load the train took time to gather speed, allowing Dino to easily run past it and onto the tracks in front of the moving carriages. Shocked, Michelangelo's cohorts at the controls slammed on the brakes and it screeched to a halt before many muffled sounds were heard from inside the carriages as several heavy and priceless pieces came loose. Michelangelo winced at the thought of the costly damage and a few disappointed billionaires.

From the tracks Dino called up to the cab. "I can offer you a deal Michelangelo", Dino proclaimed calmly, a glint in his eye as he seized the opportunity to exercise his negotiating skills.

His counterpart laughed heartily. "What on earth can you offer me? I have immortality and the gift of a great artist. As soon as these carriages reach their destinations I will also have great wealth and power. What could you possibly add to my life?" Without waiting for an answer he urged his bumbling companions to move on, making it clear he expected the train to pass directly over Dino if necessary. Fearing their master, they dutifully started up the train once more and it began to edge forward towards Dino who stood only a few yards down the track.

Dino knew he had to quicken the pace of his parley and cut to the chase. "Are you a betting man Michelangelo? I can offer you potentially a better chance."

Michelangelo laughed harder, bending double to show clearly just how much this idea had amused him. However, for a fraction of a second Dino had locked eyes with the taller man, seeing the intrigue that had hit home before his act has resumed. "What better chance can you offer me when I have the best hand?"

Dino was not convinced by his answer but he knew Michelangelo was blinded by the prospect of bringing down the church and the money and kudos that he thought that would attract. As Dino began to edge backwards away from the advancing train he knew he had no option left but to play a trump card. The only problem was, he didn't have one. He was a busted flush.

As Dino racked his brains for one last daring gamble to play, finally stepping aside to allow the train to pass, Michelangelo condescendingly waved them all off. "Thank you so much for coming to the station to bid me farewell. Most kind of you and I wish you good luck in the future…what little future you have left that is as I have it on good authority an air strike is imminent. People are just so impatient to get what they want these days. Mind you I can understand where they are coming from!"

The others could only watch as carriage after carriage hurtled past them until finally the last noisy container rumbled away. It followed

160

its linked companions through the ornate gardens and into the darkness of the secret tunnel that bore its way underneath the walls between the Vatican and Rome, finally emerging some miles east in the grounds of the Pope's sprawling private country abode.

Plaintively Dino turned to the statuesque Joan. "I just wish there was something more we could have done to stop him." he appealed to her.

Joan smiled. "Don't fret my child. We already have done more, we already have."

Dino was at first perplexed by her cryptic answer but then smiled when he saw (or rather did not see) what she meant.

Despite her sudden and deep love for her new beau, Laura was rapidly growing bored of being thrown around the inside of Leonardo's little tank as they deftly evaded the unwanted advances of their larger but more cumbersome Italian counterparts.

When she had abandoned the others and swooned over to Leonardo he had promised to devote all attention to her and covet her image through the medium of painting, endlessly studying her supine form provocatively draped by the finest silks as an assistant sustained her with grapes and small delicacies. Instead she found herself forced to sit upright in this uncomfortable craft, trying to not get her fine draperies covered in oil from the filthy exposed engine or smeared with the greasy dust that had accumulated over hundreds of years. Leonardo paid her no attention whatsoever. It turned out he was not a man but just another boy who was happier playing with his toys. She had endured this type before but she would not settle for it again. As an intelligent modern woman, Laura knew she should use dialogue to attract the attention of the would-be tank commander but time was of the essence if his tomfoolery was not to end in them being pulverized so she opted for a more direct and less time-consuming method.

Tapping Leonardo on the shoulder and whispering in his ear she urged Leonardo to look in her direction. Initially reluctant to take his eye from the opposing forces he glanced at her, rapidly performing a double take as he saw the maiden beside him was suddenly bare-chested! Almost before he could say *"Mamma mia"* Laura had convinced him to reverse the tank away from the advancing forces and a battle they could not win. Like a dog with the promise of a bone she convinced Leonardo to be led back to the Vatican buildings where he could claim the "ultimate prize" before returning to his game if that is what he wished. She hoped it would not have to go that far though and he would just follow long enough for her to find her new friends and use the promise to enlist his help to focus on the power-crazed Michelangelo once more.

Alice knew exactly why she had crept onto the moving train but she did not know what she could do on her own to stop Michelangelo even if the urge to try was overpowering. She sat crouched inside one of the train carriages, seeing only the dim outlines of the eerie wrapped statues and busts that loomed over her in the semi-darkness. All she could hear was the muffled *clickety-clack* of the wheels rumbling over the tracks and the creaks of the hollow container that was reluctantly hauled along. Laura knew she needed a course of action and that she could not remain in her hiding place indefinitely. Exposed in the container she would be seen as soon as the side was opened to remove the goods. But then, after noticing a carelessly secured statuette wobble after they rounded a curve at a precarious speed, she knew exactly what she was going to do.

With their leader Leonardo gone, his lieges also lost faith and scattered, Isaac Newton the last to stay, throwing the last few explosive apples before he too scuttled away. The baffled and disbelieving Italian troops advanced now without resistance, bridging the moat with a makeshift crossing, rapidly gaining control of St. Peter's square. Given the all clear from the heavy guns, the infantry now flowed into the open space like ants fanning out in regimented lines. The physical battle seemingly over they removed all traces that the Swiss guards had been there, pulling down the Swiss flags that had been hoisted in triumph only minutes earlier. The square deemed safe, the troops made a tentative incursion into the first of the buildings that encircled the square underneath the curved colonnade. Moving systematically from room to room, they quizzed anyone they found at gunpoint on the whereabouts of the flamboyant man in the strange tank, the one they assumed to be the leader of this bizarre uprising but none of the clerical staff they found seemed to know his location or they were too scared to share. Onward the forces cantered, deeper and deeper into the heart of the Vatican in search of their quarry.

Leonardo was clearly a sated man as he sauntered with Laura toward the Vatican railway station. "Sorry we're late," beamed the jovial Leonardo, sporting what he considered to be a winning smile, the edges of his mouth softened by his scruffy beard. "What have we missed?"

Joan raised her considerable eyebrows towards the taller man like a headmistress about to scold one of her unruly children. "What you have *missed* is your former ally fleeing the scene with all the Vatican's treasures!"

The smile was wiped from his face. "He is no friend of mine anymore, I can assure you of that. Where did that little man go?" he asked almost theatrically.

"He has already left us on the Pope's personal train, heading to the papal country estate. We have no chance of catching him before he disperses the Vatican treasures and disappears to God knows where on a private jet."

Leonardo stroked his beard thoughtfully. "Oh I wouldn't be so sure of that my dear."

"Oh, no," Joan said with sudden despair. "You are not thinking what I *think* you are thinking are you?"

"Well, my glorious bird has never taken to the air but I think it might be high time for it to dust off its feathers for its maiden flight. After all, I have performed the calculations. There is no *mathematical* reason why it should not work."

"You are a fool Leonardo and you always have been. If these two want to risk their lives then it's up to them. Myself, I will have no part of it. She turned to face her two remaining followers. "I have guided you this far my children but what you do now is of your own willing. I just hope you choose the right path."

Dino chose to address Joan. "I don't care about Michelangelo or anything apart from Alice. We must find a way to rescue her so for that reason alone I will climb on board."

"Excellent!" Responded Leonardo. Follow me and we will set off forthwith. There is obviously no time to lose!"

Caught up in the moment, not one of them had remembered that quiet Luca was no longer in their group. He was already a forgotten nobody, in their view an also-ran in this particular race for survival.

Michelangelo hated confined spaces, so naturally he was more than pleased to finally emerge from the long tunnel and back into the blinding light of the Lazio hills outside Rome. Passively he looked over at the overweight and hairy driver that sat (luckily not too closely) beside him, bemoaning what gross bloated shapes the human body could assume. He would certainly not be writing one of his sonnets of love in his honour.

He turned to view the scene ahead once again, a bucolic vista that flashed towards and past the train, cleansing his eyes. Then the serenity of his mood was shattered as they traversed a gentle curve in the track and a loud rumbling sound emanated from one of the numerous carriages they towed. Disturbed by the unexpected reverberation, Michelangelo looked into the rear-view mirror just in time to see a ghostly shape awkwardly tumbling away and back along the track. Then, a second object bounced irregularly on the rails and broke in two before the segments embedded themselves into the soft verge.

Michelangelo ordered his burly assistants to stop the train post haste and made them run back along the length of the train to investigate. He fumed, realizing his idiots must have not locked one of the carriage doors properly and a couple of the statues must have broken loose of their moorings and wobbled out onto the track as they went round the last bend. He reasoned that at least he would be able to dispose of those useless creatures very soon.

164

The artist stewed for a couple of minutes in the stained and uncomfortable passenger seat before he realized that he had not seen or heard his two assistants for longer than was required to ascertain the problem and report back. What were those dullards doing, he wondered. Unfastening his seat belt, he pivoted his body to peer out of the open passenger window and back down the side of the train. Still he could see nothing. He retracted his head, eager to step out and reprimand his sluggish cohorts but before his bonce had returned to where his body resided in the cab, he felt a constriction around his neck as a pair of slender legs wrapped themselves around him like a boa constrictor, threatening to cut off his cranial blood supply. Naturally he struggled to free himself but the action only increased the pressure on his neck. Oddly, the last thoughts that went through the renaissance villain's mind before he slipped into unconsciousness was how shapely the calves were and what a fine model they would make for a marble statue of the same proportions.

Meanwhile, having descended back down to the subterranean bowls of the Vatican, Dino and Laura were as cautious as a couple about to buy a cheap run-about from a used-car salesman.

"Is this thing safe?" said Dino with more than a hint of incredulity.

"My boy, you hurt me with these words," replied Leonardo, pretending to be mortally offended. "My beautiful contraption will embrace you securely in its bosom and not rock you from its berth. No, it will fly more serenely and safely than any gliding raptor!"

Sadly, Dino's scepticism was not quelled by the flamboyant man's impassioned guarantee so the master again attempted to reassure his young compatriot. "Here, let me show you. I must warn you to stand back though, once these blades start to rotate they can whip up quite a fearsome wind!" With a boyhood smile plastered on his face, Leonardo placed himself into the cockpit of the early helicopter.

Dino obeyed and stood back next to Laura. They exchanged glances with eyebrows raised and arms firmly crossed, both equally unsure they desired to risk their lives with another invention from the Renaissance man.

Leonardo was now engrossed with his machine, flitting around the contraption with nimble swiftness as he adjusted an array of intricate wooden switches before hurling himself into one of the elaborately carved seats and pounding the peddles in the foot well. Initially the energy transferred from the legs of the immortal failed to spark the ancient aircraft into life but after much exertion and perspiration, the rotor blades reluctantly creaked into motion. Leonardo laughed with relief as they span faster and faster, the effort required to turn the now rapidly spinning planks obviously less than it was at the initial transition from inertia to movement.

The two reluctant passengers looked on with some surprise at the graceful oscillation of the gently curved protrusions that resembled sycamore wing nuts as they carved through the air to create lift that now caused the craft to bob up and down, straining against its heavy sandbag moorings like a fly trying to buzz away from an adhesive spider's web. In the end, a little verbal encouragement was all that was required for the duo to hop tentatively into the graceful flying craft. Without instruction, Dino immediately helped out Leonardo by pounding the pedals at his feet as Laura reached overboard to unfasten the sandbag weights. As the last rope hit the basement floor the wooden helicopter jerkily took off, listing at first but then steadying as Leonardo adjusted a lever or two. The two men on board were now enjoying the sensation of man-powered flight but for Laura the experience was already making her feel more than a little queasy and so she reclined as best she could in the solitary back seat. She too had pedals in her foot-well but a combination of nausea, expensive shoes and the risk of unsightly perspiration meant she opted to leave that job to the boys in the front.

Up they rose in what approximated to a vertical direction, soaring towards the great ceiling that once again parted to let them pass straight through the hitherto solid foundations of St. Peter's square, no evidence remaining of the mysterious canal that had appeared earlier from within that divide. However, on this occasion, instead of stopping at ground level, they continued their ascent above the bemused tanks that followed their trajectory with their gun turrets inclining at the same pace until their restricted trunks could not follow any longer.   Unfortunately for the passengers in the medieval flying machine, another branch of the combined armed forces were not so hesitant to open fire. The perilously placed occupants heard this new danger well before they saw them, their burgeoning presence heralded by a thunderous and foreboding rumbling that cut through the sky before the sight of three sleek fighter planes approaching at great haste from the east.

The fragile wooden craft would be no match for the state of the art warplanes so naturally all aboard were petrified when the planes opened fire in a rapid burst from their guns. Even the hitherto unflappable Leonardo appeared alarmed although he was not hesitant in his response as he immediately stopped pedalling and pulled a small red lever to his side. The blades above their heads stopped spinning an in instant before rapidly furling like an umbrella inverting in high winds. Suddenly shorn of its aerodynamics the craft plummeted through the air as the ammunition from the enemy aircraft whistled harmlessly overhead. The solid ground loomed before them but as the passengers instinctively (if pointlessly) braced themselves for what would be a deadly impact, Leonardo began to peddle furiously once more as he pulled another lever that unfurled the rotating blades but at a more askew angle than before. Now instead of regaining height, they travelled forwards through the air, barely thirty feet above the ground. Too low for the fast airplanes to target them safely and now out of reach of the tanks, they were able to skim above the now open and undulating terrain of the Vatican gardens.

"That was close. Too close," Leonardo muttered almost more to himself than anyone else. "We need to get out of here before they decide to use their heat–seeking missiles."

Without the need for a further prompt, Dino pressed heavily on his peddles once more, propelling the craft surprisingly quickly over the grounds, past the maze where the spilt blood of the late Pope was still visible seeping out from underneath one of the manicured hedges then above the colonnaded boundaries and out of the tiny state and back into Italian airspace. In seconds they crossed the no-man's land between the two sparring nations, the rolls of barbed wire rimmed by a squadron of young, scared infantry. The 'green' troops did not even notice the almost soundless primitive helicopter passing just over their protective helmets but they did hear the rumbling sound of the warplanes turning back towards them. The occupants of the flying machine also detected the now familiar rumble but they knew they were out of harm's way.

The trio zigzagged above the side streets to muster as little attention as possible before heading to the Tiber. Here they followed the course of the mighty river for some time and then veered away from the city and towards the Pope's villa in the gently rolling Alban hills in the near distance. To avoid detection from above, the craft maintained its low altitude flight path although this did mean being in close proximity to curious pedestrians and passing vehicles on the ground. Whilst most gawped or waved, thinking they were watching a record attempt in progress or perhaps the latest blockbuster movie being filmed, some youths hurled objects at the odd-looking flying device. The juveniles did manage to reach their target on occasion but luckily the only material damage was to Laura's dress from a deftly thrown egg.

Apart from the occasional airborne irritant, the flight was now largely trouble free and the passengers all used the relative calm to take stock of their relative situations.

Laura looked at the man in front of her at the controls – her latest infatuation. Was he yet another poor choice or could she really spend the rest of her days with him in happiness, ageing and finally dying as he kept his beauty and youthful vigour?

Dino looked on at Laura – the woman who had spurned him although now he held no bitterness towards her. He knew that for him the thrill of the chase was the biggest aphrodisiac and now that had ended he would find another, never venturing back to the last for fear of wasting emotion or time. After all, he knew he could never find anyone to match his greatest love – himself.

Ahead of them a plain but palatial building crept into view from over the horizon, its vast structure normally inconspicuous as it was nestled into a hillside depression and surrounded by ramshackle old farmhouses and served by a single track railway line. But today the structure was made more evident by virtue of a surrounding ring of colourful Swiss guards. On spotting the welcoming committee, Leonardo altered the course of the craft to head directly towards

168

them, a grim determination now etched on his bearded face.

Michelangelo awoke tetchily from his imposed slumber with a bright sun streaming through the large windscreen in front of him. Instinctively he tried to raise his hands to cover his eyes from the glare but he found his arms would not obey as they were firmly restrained against his side by thick tape that also secured him to the passenger seat. Straining his neck, he awkwardly looked over to the driver's seat to see Alice had commandeered the train, eyes fixed on the track ahead.

"You've put on weight since I last saw you," he said flippantly.

Alice looked at Michelangelo and then down at her midriff, noting that her bump had expanded yet again and now clearly strained against the fabric of her top. For a moment, she quelled her lack of understanding at how rapidly her body was changing. "Nice to see you too!" she retorted sarcastically.

Michelangelo wrestled with his bonds unsuccessfully and lost his sense of humour. "Are my assistants safe?" he barked.

"Yes, they are fine. They will have sore heads in the morning and a rather long walk ahead of them though."

Michelangelo sighed. "You know you can't stop me, don't you? If I don't arrive at the villa my troops will carry on with my strict instructions to freight all the church's precious artefacts around the world to their pre-allotted buyers." He wished he could flamboyantly swing his arms to illustrate his words but he thought he adequately got his point across.

"Oh I am fully aware of that. To be honest I am not interested in the demise of the church, what you do with any trophy they owned, or even who might own them next. I am a dancer Mr. Michelangelo. That is what I do, that is all I have wanted to do and why I was lured to the Vatican in the first place under false pretences. Although, don't get me wrong, I can envisage personal benefits from the downfall of the Vatican. The Catholic Church always denounces the type of expressive dance I love as little more than a prelude to fornication.

Without their pious attitude pervading mainstream thought I will be freer to create and perform to wider audiences without judgment.

"So why, if you appear to be on my side, have you commandeered my train and restrained me so?"

"Because I needed some time alone with you to offer you a deal and I feared you would not listen to me without being a captive audience."

Michelangelo laughed haughtily. "A *deal*? With *you*? Here we go again. What could you possibly offer me?"

Solemnly Alice responded. "What I could offer you is getting Leonardo off your back. He won't let you off for double-crossing him and I know a way of ensuring he will not trouble you again."

Michelangelo stopped laughing, his face now pallid and drawn. "Ok. I don't know why but something makes me believe you. Tell me my pregnant dancer, what is your cunning plan and what do you want in return?"

"There is one thing I should probably tell you both…" said Leonardo as his flying machine began its descent to the ground.

"And pray tell what might that be?" replied a now impatient Dino.

"I have never had a successful landing with this thing…so please brace yourselves!"

The trio duly prepared themselves for a bumpy landing as the gently rolling hillside below the villa loomed up towards them at an uncomfortable pace. Despite the best efforts of the flamboyant pilot, the landing was jolting at best and bone jarring at worst. On impact the front of the wooden structure dug into the soft turf pivoting the whole craft up and over, ejecting its occupants as it plopped onto its fragile rotating blades.

Picking themselves up, they silently began the short walk up to the barricaded main gates of the villa. Leonardo walked confidently, his body language giving assurances he did not foresee any problems gaining entry to the Pope's lavish summer residence. Inwardly he felt very different but he was fairly sure a solution would somehow present itself before very long.

As they neared the guarded front gate, a rumbling behind their right shoulders signalled the arrival of a train along the tracks that emerged from a tunnel at their side, just outside the perimeter walls. Immediately they recognized the sleek livery of the engine cab and its snake-like body of adjoined wagons that stretched into the distance. Laura and Dino resisted the urge to run over to see if Alice was still on board and safe and well somewhere inside. They knew any rash movement may be seen as aggressive by the nervous trigger-happy guards who were already raising their weapons defensively as they strode forwards to greet both the train and the unwelcome visitors. One of the guards hopped up onto the cab of the train to speak to the driver.

Alice was uncomfortable as she crouched out of sight in the driver's foot well with a elbow poised threateningly within a couple of inches of Michelangelo's nether regions. She had already warned him she would use her full force on the delicate area if he showed any sign of alerting the guards of her presence and therefore reneging on the deal they had made. With only a hint of nervous perspiration on his brow he did not arouse any suspicions in the guard who popped his head into the cab briefly for a quick look. Not seeing anything untoward, he allowed them to enter the grounds of the great villa.

The train was waved onward and it slowly trundled towards the walls and then through as the great stone barrier parted to allow its passage. Looking on, Leonardo pondered that their entry would not be so simple. But then, with a sudden flash of inspiration, he realized how they would also all get past the sullen guards with ease. Brazenly he stepped up to the one who appeared to be their commander and opened what he hoped would be a friendly line of dialogue. The commander stepped forward in a defensive but openly curious manner.

"Capitano!" said the artist, offering his hand that was flatly rejected with healthy suspicion by the soldier.

"I am a *Generale* actually, but I understand that the stars on my lapel are difficult to determine at first so I will let that insult slide.

What business do you and your cronies have here at the Pope's private villa? I assume you were not thinking of trying to enter?"

In mock shock at his comment, Leonardo crossed his hands over his chest. "Heavens forbid and my apologies *Generale*. No, we have absolutely no intention of entering the grand papal residence. We have just come here on a tourist trip to admire the fine buildings and the wonderful scenery. I only came to talk to you to bid you good day and we will shortly be on our way." Leonardo appeared to be good to his word as he began to walk away, his steps followed closely by the eyes of the still sceptical army commander. However, after no more than half a dozen footsteps he stopped, appeared to think for a second and then turned back to the commander who, along with the men in his immediate vicinity, visibly bristled at the sudden re-advancement.

Leonardo addressed the rankled general once more. "There is just one thing you could do for us before we move on though if you would be so kind?"

"And what might that be?" replied the general, slightly amused but beginning to grow a little bored of this obviously simple (but oddly familiar looking) eccentric dandy.

"Well, we are all parched after a long walk and we neglected to bring enough liquid refreshment with us. So we were wondering if we could all perhaps have a sip from your canteens of water?"

The commander narrowed his eyes. He had been trained never to be out-thought by sneaky adversaries but surely this bizarre little man was harmless enough. Without saying another word (but without ever taking his eyes off the well dressed man) he unhooked his own army regulation water pouch and hurled it towards the visitor, its contents audibly sloshing around the interior as it flew through the air.

Leonardo deftly caught the bladder shaped vessel and nodded his gratitude as he unscrewed the lid, pursing his lips to receive the clear liquid efficiently from the small aperture. However he had only swallowed a few drops before he doubled over, spraying the contents of what he had ingested out onto the grass in front of him. He now held the pouch out in front of him, scrutinizing each side as if closer inspection of the container would belie its unexpected contents.

"Why, this is not water, its wine! Normally I would not be grateful but this will hardly quench my thirst on a hot day such as this!"

"Give me that!" demanded the unbelieving senior officer as he snatched back the open pouch. He tried to look inside before sniffing the contents through the neck of the padded flask. Finally he took a tentative sip and then a deep gulp. *My God, it* was *wine* he thought, *and very good wine at that!* Suddenly forgetting he was on duty, he tipped back the flask, draining the contents of the container of its velvety red and intoxicating fluid. Finally sated he re-affixed the cap and was about to return the flask to its fixing on his waist when he heard a familiar sloshing sound. *It can't be possible, I drained the flask!* The squadron leader opened the stopper once more. To his amazement, the flask was full to the brim! He knew he should resist but he could not help himself from knocking back more of the luscious ruby-red wine.

The soldiers to each side of him watched intently before finally scrabbling to retrieve their own flasks, furiously pawing at the lids in eager anticipation. They too found their flasks to contain the same wine! As they began to drink deeply, their commander was already beginning to feel the effects, laughing as he lost control of his legs, falling onto the ground like an ungainly toddler. The message spread along the lines of troops, flasks being raised to mouths and dropped again in a sinuous Mexican wave. Before long the entire brigade was lazing on the grass as they drank and told tales, some even play fighting – to a man forgetting the nature of their instructions or not caring if they did.

Leonardo politely doffed his cap as he walked around the sluggish forms and through the ornate stone gateway, gesturing his companions to follow him into the now unprotected courtyard.

III-III – THE PAPAL VILLA

Leonardo stepped through to the inner courtyard behind the villa walls where a semi-circle of gravel lined by ornate gardens led the eye to a simple looking white building that more resembled council offices than the getaway of the head of the Roman Catholic Church. This incongruity was lost on Leonardo though as himself, Laura and Dino focused on the figures of Alice and Michelangelo who stood between them and the papal holiday home. As Leonardo stood and glowered, his companions ran to greet Alice but they stopped just short of an embrace when they saw her unmistakable abdominal swelling. They were almost speechless but Dino finally found some words. "What on earth has happened to you?" he delicately posed.

"A very good question Dino. This morning I was two weeks pregnant but today...well you can see for yourself!" she replied, stroking her prominent bump as she bent herself backwards to temporarily ease her aching spine.

Dino's pleasure at seeing Alice was tempered suddenly as it sunk in who was by her side. "Why are you now standing side by side with *him*?" he said with derision. "So this is your grand plan? A selfish one to save yourself?"

Alice looked down briefly as if momentarily ashamed but she soon regained full eye contact with the swarthy southerner. "Things change Dino, as you can very well see," she said, stroking her large bump once more. "I decided that it is the time in my life when I need to be selfish and think about how I can best provide for my new child. I will not be able to pursue a career as a dancer now so I will have to do the next best thing. Michelangelo has decided to employ me. Despite my burgeoning middle I am still as agile as I was before and he has therefore agreed to use my otherworldly skills as a bodyguard to protect him from unwarranted advances that before the Vatican's treasures are safely airborne. In return, he has agreed to pay me one percent of the revenue from the sales. That money I will use to set up a chain of dance academies across Italy and then the western world so I can live the dream that I never realized, if now only vicariously though my pupils."

Dino laughed, feeling like he was in an old Wild West film. "You as a bodyguard? In that condition? You wouldn't be able to protect him from a wasp let alone a trained assassin!"

A flicker of doubt crossed the young girl's face, almost like a poker tell, before she responded with vigour. "Try me," she said simply.

Dino laughed a little more but stopped when he saw she was serious. He would never purposefully hurt a woman physically but this little madam maybe needed to be put in her place. A playful jab to each arm he thought would be ample for her misplaced bravado to surely evaporate. Confidently Dino stepped forward in a boxer's stance. Alice remained motionless as he stepped within reach of the pregnant woman before quickly thrusting forward a fist, calculated to just make contact with her upper arm, the lightest of touches. To his amazement, his punch never got close and was rapidly enclosed by Alice's hand. Clasped in place, she used Dino's fist as a pivot that allowed a foot to come swinging through the air, connecting painfully with the side of his head, causing his left ear to throb. His pride hurt more than this ear though as Alice let him go and retreated, crossing her arms and allowing herself a subtle smile in triumph.

Stepping between the sparring partners, Michelangelo interjected. "Enough of these childish squabbles! Listen, I have no time for this. It is nice to see you all again," he said insincerely, "But I really have a plane to catch. I'm afraid if you had some grandiose but ultimately poorly hatched scheme to stop me or my treasures leaving then I am afraid to say you are far too late. Soon the Pope will address the world again, automatically and simultaneously broadcasting to all television channels in the world. I suggest you find a television somewhere my friends as believe me, this will be well worth watching as there is one last surprise in store! Anyway, I as said, now I must bid you all farewell!" With that, the artist turned away from the group, his new and now very pregnant bodyguard in tow although he only walked a few steps before he half-turned on his heel for an obviously well rehearsed footnote. "I must add though, despite my obvious joy at the downfall of the Catholic Church and the gargantuan increase in my own personal wealth and influence, I did expect the church and you, its chosen emissaries, to put up much more of a resistance. Of all of you it was only Alice here who showed any semblance of skill or tactical nous and that backfired on the rest of you when she chose to join me!"

"You know I cannot claim to speak on behalf of the church Michelangelo" said Leonardo. "And my quest to defeat you has been a personal one, ever since you decided to leave me to rot in that miniature world of plastic figures and tiny trains instead of sharing the immense wealth and power you now hold on your own. But rest assured, if you *are* able to leave today, myself or others will muster forces to hunt you down and vanquish the megalomaniac you have become. It is true that only Alice has shown any worthy skills so far but her speedy pregnancy surely shows higher forces have something in store for her that yet may thwart your goals."

Michelangelo laughed but looked uneasily at Alice, hoping he would be well out of the way before any screaming child would be born. He knew a baby could not do anything to harm him though, beyond dulling his concentration with its constant whining despite Leonardo's half- baked foretelling of those new "special" births that would surely occur this year on the cusp of the mysterious 23-year cycle.

"Let me make you a deal my old adversary," continued Leonardo. "Each one of us will have one last opportunity to prove we have been empowered mysteriously by the Vatican to end your plundering reign. If we win, you can still leave with your life intact but we demand to know the exact destinations of the Vatican's assets that are already airborne so that we can work to return them. If we fail, then you carry on but we ask you also let us go freely."

"And If I refuse?"

"I will use my trebuchets and catapults to shoot down your chartered planes and their purloined goods and you will be at the mercy of hundreds of very angry millionaires and billionaires who I am sure would not be best amused if they do not receive what they have all paid so much for".

Michelangelo swallowed hard at the unpalatable thought of a plague of well-resourced billionaires on his tail, shaking his head to clear the mind of the unwanted image. "You are bluffing! Either that or you are all mad. There is no way your weapons could be that accurate or powerful!"

Leonardo raised his eyebrows as if surprised that his statement had been questioned. "You don't believe me my old colleague?"

Michelangelo stood cockily with his hands clasped behind his back. "Ok. I have a big ego and I have time before the bumbling Italian forces happen to stumble upon where we are. I will entertain your little charade. Bring it on, who will attempt to defeat me first?" he said, rubbing his hands, sure of victory but also equally keen for this mildly amusing distraction to not take up too much time.

"Ladies first I think", said Laura, defiantly stepping forward.

Leonardo nodded his head and ushered Laura and Michelangelo towards a small door in the side of the villa, like a ringmaster encouraging wary punters into a circus show. "Come with me through this door into what appears to be a normal room but I assure you soon it will be anything but."

"Please, after you," said Michelangelo with healthy scepticism as he opened the door for his female companion. In she glided, followed by the immortal artist turned villain.

The door closed solidly behind them and the room was pitch black. Michelangelo lost Laura immediately, in fact he could not even see the hand he held in front of him as he gingerly stepped into the void. In time the complete darkness eased by a degree as a soft rosy glow began to emanate from one corner of the room, a red light shining from behind a thin translucent material, the glow increasing in intensity as slowly as a morning sunrise. Soon the vague contours of a shrouded shape could be discerned, the edges becoming more defined as the brightness continued to intensify. The gently undulating landscape soon belied the familiar shape of a supine female figure. Michelangelo could not help but subconsciously lick his lips. He presumed the shape was that of Laura, the smooth lines suggesting she was naked. His natural instincts were to move closer and pull back the silken drape that billowed languidly between them but he was reluctant to lose the initiative, aware that everything was probably not as it seemed. He did not want to lose this game through a rash decision influenced by any physical desire...not that he had been told the rules or how to play.

"I don't know why you are bothering to try to defeat me with your wiles my dear," he said. "You are undoubtedly one of the most beautiful creatures I have ever seen in all my many years and therefore quite a distraction but I am afraid beauty will always come second to power and influence in terms of what I find most attractive. Besides, your physical attraction to me is largely an appreciation of beauty in a professional and artistic endeavour, my personal desires of the flesh are more generally directed in another direction."

The figure beneath the shroud responded. "I thought as much Michelangelo, but what if you could harness and be in control of the *power* of beauty?"

A peculiar draught of wind snaked past Michelangelo's lower legs and on to the shroud, its small force just enough to momentarily peel back a corner of the swaying silken screen, revealing Laura's delicate feet and lower legs. The light olive-hued skin was uncovered, the legs crossed and resting on a plush upholstered chaise-long. Before the artist could fully devour the scene with his eyes, the draft subsided, obscuring her legs once more.

He caught his breath before replying. "I can see what you are trying to do but you forget what era I was from Laura. I knew Machiavelli well and I have studied his predecessor Sun Tzu and his many successors. It is obvious you are foolishly trying to use the *laws of power* on me. You think you are clever, concealing your real intentions and saying less than is necessary but courting attention at all costs. You use yourself as bait to get me to come towards you, hoping to win through your actions rather than argument and being generous in an attempt to disarm me. You have appealed to my self-interests in a friendly manner when really you are playing for the other side. Here behind this shroud you assume formlessness, creating compelling spectacles with the illusionist assistance of Leonardo. You are right to an extent but not entirely correct. You have forgotten some key aspects of the way they work and must be applied though. I must be a fool to be vanquished and I assure you I am not. Here you have offended the wrong person and I do not think

178

you have planned your moves far enough ahead. This was an error but not your greatest one. *That* was not actually a mistake of your choosing but an accident of nature. You are unaware of the most important law of all young lady, *never* appear perfect!" With that he ran forward and yanked the curtain back to reveal Laura's form. However, instead of gazing on her body made up of flesh and bones, he saw the shape of her form consisted of a mass of numbers of different colours and size. The figures pulsed in her chest before bursting forth, flowing around her 'body' to the very extremities of her limbs, the numbers decreasing in value and size as they coursed until they slowed and turned back towards the figurative pumping heart, their hues altering as they slid and bumped past each other. Michelangelo knew this was a mere illusion but he could not help to be awed by the imagery, wondering if there was a Sumerian influence. Man equals one and woman equals two and so forth.

Below him, the mass of flowing numbers spoke with Laura's voice. "You are right in some of what you say," said the numerical Laura, each spoken word joined by a cascade of numbers ejected from the mouth, each one rapidly falling in value to zero before disappearing. "Although my perfection is *not* my downfall but rather my winning hand which I am willing to share with you if you accept certain conditions. There is power in perfection but it is short lived as man has always feared it. Look at the Ancient Greeks as an example. They sought faultlessness in the statues of their gods but they became scared when they made them too real, too life-like. They felt the stone pupils of the eyes watching them as they walked past the figures and thought the imitations would come to life and murder them all as they slept. Today we have the same fears in a different form with computers that mirror our brains. Perhaps in the near future robots will realize the fears of both these components together. Little did the ancient Greeks know they were on the threshold of releasing the secret of nature."

Michelangelo laughed. "There are patterns to be found in nature but there are no secrets and no code. Who is it that created the numbers and systems for these patterns to appear? Why it is man who is always in control of his environment and therefore of nature itself."

"But are we not still a part of nature and bound by its laws? Just one species like the millions of others that have followed before, their numbers rising but then inevitably falling as nature imposes its restrictions?"

"No, we are different. We are the conquerors of nature and nowadays we do not fear perfection but strive to achieve it. Through our collective intelligence we can bend nature to our laws and we will not be tied by the confines of our environment but break beyond it and out into the great bounds of space. If man cannot achieve this as a whole, it will be myself and the other chosen ones who will still thrive!" Michelangelo felt he had won this battle and bent down to touch the bright red numbers that formed the heart of the numerical creature. As he did so, Michelangelo was bathed in ever-growing crimson shapes before the shape of Laura disassembled, flowing away to nothing like a boiling liquid dispersing and then evaporating before his eyes.

Darkness enveloped Michelangelo once more until an upright hollow rectangle of light appeared and pulsed, bordering the door through which he could leave. He strode out to meet the others. "One down, two to go," he triumphantly exclaimed. "Who will be next to test their mental skills against me?"

Dino stepped forward. "My turn your honour," he mocked before whispering some instructions into Leonardo's ear. The artist nodded and then smiled before ushering both of the players into the mysterious room as a crest-fallen Laura looked on, struggling to reconcile the idea of her perfection as a fault.

Dino passed through the doorway, followed by Michelangelo. Immediately a fierce light blinded the older man and instinctively he shielded his eyes from the damaging glare. Once his eyes adjusted, he peered out from between his watery eyelids. He could see he was in a dirt street in a small town with ramshackle timber-built buildings. It was dry and dusty and a hot wind blew from his left to his right, a breeze strong enough to carry dust, sand and even the odd tumbleweed. Across the road there was just one building, a well-used drinking hole that looked as though it had been uprooted straight from an old Western film. There was no one to be seen as

Michelangelo boldly walked over to the swinging doors, pushing them inwards as he entered the bar.

Inside the scene was exactly as he expected. Small tables were scattered across the sawdust-covered floor at his feet, three or four men sitting at each one. Every grizzled character was a subtle variation on a theme – unshaven and dirty with a drink, a gun and a jealously clasped fan of dog-eared playing cards. None of the players acknowledged his presence, seemingly too engrossed in their games. At the back of the room, a balcony overhung a tired piano that teetered on three legs. Stood on the balcony was the only thing of colour in the whole place, a brilliant scarlet dress worn by a bored madam waiting for one of the card players to get drunk enough (or temporarily rich enough) to want to pause their playing and indulge a more carnal urge.

Michelangelo smiled at the rich visual tapestry. He had to admit Leonardo had outdone himself with this particular illusion, as it was certainly far more complex than the first. It was then he spotted Dino over to his left, acting as the barman, polishing a glass with a dirty rag and the application of a little spit and elbow grease.

Removing the large hat he found to be on the top of his head, Michelangelo placed it on the bar and Dino turned his attention away from the filthy vessel.

"What can I get you," Dino the barman asked gruffly.

"What's good here?"

"Oh it's all good," Dino replied with false pride. "But the more you risk, the better the potential rewards!" he said, trying to tempt the other man with an over-exaggerated wink.

"So what exactly are you offering me young man?"

"Simple. I am offering you a choice. You can turn away now and the door will reappear. I will lose my chance and Leonardo will have the final chance to beat you. However, you will never know what deal I had on the table for you. Alternatively, you can play me at my little game and obviously risk losing."

Michelangelo squinted at the other man. "I will play your game. Deal the cards my little southerner."

"Oh this is not a game of cards, it is something far more ancient than that. It is a game of chance that dates back to the great civilizations of ancient China if not from even more primitive days." Without further explanation, Dino the barman reached beneath the bar and produced three scratched wooden cups, barely larger than eggcups. He placed them upside-down on the bar top in a neat row, a few inches apart. From the pocket of his dusty and stained denim trousers, he retrieved a small ball that he placed alongside the cups.

With Michelangelo nodding his acceptance of the challenge, Dino openly placed the ball under the middle cup. The pair had now attracted an audience as many of the grizzled patrons abandoned their games of cards, crowding around the two men, each one craning their necks to get the best angle of the strange duel.

Nimbly Dino moved the cups around each other, their movements like a pair of mating snakes, the wooden surfaces of cup and bar grating against each other until finally the motion stopped with the cups in a new formation. Standing back, he opened his palms, soundlessly prompting Michelangelo to make his choice of which cup the ball now resided beneath. Without hesitation, he tapped the cup on his right and Dino's left. Dino looked surprised at his choice. "Are you sure my adversary?" he theatrically asked.

"Deadly sure," he responded coldly.

Tentatively Dino lifted the chosen cup to indeed reveal the ball sitting underneath. Feigning despair he made a plaintive offer. "Best of three?"

Michelangelo made a short snorting sound before deciding to play along. "Ok. Very well, best of three," he spat, knowing full well the easy start was all part of the act.

Dino again showed the other man the small ball before once more placing it underneath the middle cup. Michelangelo ignored the leagued foul breath of the watching crowd that wafted over his shoulder, the masses stepping ever closer to gain a better view of the challenge. He remained transfixed on the moving cups, following every move of the one that contained the ball. Dino was faster this time, much faster in fact but as long as nothing broke his concentration, he would be able to track the small sphere, even when Dino attempted to conceal the cups with his intertwining forearms.

But from high above on the balcony a distraction duly arrived. "Happy hour!" shrieked the madam of the house. "Every girl now half price until sundown!" The mass of viewers behind Michelangelo hollered as one, arms and hats moving in front of the immortal artist as they all clamoured for the wide staircase as one, each of them intent on grabbing their favourite wench before a fellow down-and-out fastened on to their favoured filly first.

The flailing arms were a brief disruption but just long enough to obstruct Michelangelo's view for a crucial split-second. When he could see clearly again, the cups were stationary. Dino looked up and gestured for the player to again pick his cup.

"I believe," said the older man as he scrutinized each cup closely, "That the ball is not sitting under any of the cups!"

Dino looked a little too surprised. "That is a quite a dangerous guess. Can I ask why you would think such a thing?"

"I do not think it was coincidence for the madam up there to suddenly offer a discount of her charges. You knew that such an offer would create a scene down here amongst this surly crowd, providing the distraction you needed to remove the ball."

"Very impressive. On that score you are right but the challenge of this part of the game is to tell me where it is."

"Well, I know it is not behind the bar as that would be far too obvious. My best guess is that at the moment my vision was temporarily blocked you hurled the ball up to the madam here who gathered it in the pleats of her long dress before secreting it about her person." Michelangelo looked up to the larger than life brothel manager.

On the balcony the madam had been listening in, arms crossed over the low balustrade as her large but aging breasts threatened to break free of their moorings and spill over the edge. "To you my love I am not *The Madam* but Ms. Moonrise if you please. Although if you get to know me a little better you can call me Scarlett," she said with a well-practiced wink as she produced the ball from some mysterious cavity beneath her petticoat, throwing it back down to Dino.

Dino looked sheepish. "I am sorry, I admit I was not playing fair and square but I think that makes us even in more ways than one. I promise you there will be no tricks for the all-important decider. Just a pure battle of skills and may the best man win!" Dino reset the cups, this time placing the ball under the left-hand receptacle from Michelangelo's perspective.

Again Dino weaved his hands over the cups, the scraping noise increasing in frequency and intensity as the upturned vessels oscillated ever faster. Michelangelo at first followed with ease but soon lost sight of the cup with the ball as Dino moved so fast that the cups and his hands became a blur of beige.

Suddenly Dino stopped, prompting Michelangelo to choose his cup. He had no idea which one contained the ball so made a fearless guess at the middle cup. Without ceremony, Dino lifted the middle cup to reveal the ball. Michelangelo clapped his hands together with glee and was about to mock the other man but he was stopped by Dino holding up an index finger, urging him to pause. Maintaining eye contact, Dino lifted up the cup to the left and then the one to the right, revealing an identical ball to the first beneath each one. "You forget the rules of where you are my venerable artist. In this created world I was able to move the ball so fast that I could treat it as if it was a single particle of light. In here I am able to demonstrate that matter and energy can display characteristics of both waves and particles. The ball split into three separate objects and occupied the three cups simultaneously. Although, in actuality, it was the same one ball in three different places. In this way I show you how the power of one person can be multiplied with the help of others. A collective working together will always be victorious over the needs and the wants of the single person."

Michelangelo looked on sagely. "Some would call that a trick but I will accept that as a win to you. Besides, I would have been disappointed if any of you had succeeded before I met with the master, Leonardo. I cannot accept your argument though. Look at

184

history my friend. It is littered with the achievements of the single determined man or woman winning against the masses."

Michelangelo left the dusty drinking-hole to the dull rhythmic thumping of the patrons enjoying 'happy hour' upstairs. He pushed open the swinging doors and back out into the light and thankfully real physical rules of modern day.

Leonardo smiled as he saw his old friend turned foe. "So, I *do* get my chance after all. Let us return back to the room for your final test."

Michelangelo's heart raced with anticipation at what may lay ahead in his final and surely most testing challenge.

He did not like what he saw though as he stepped through the doors. "Ah, the scene of my recent incarceration, how very kind of you to bring me back to my temporary home that I grew to know so well." He said sarcastically.

"I have taken the liberty of making a few changes to your house though if you would like to step inside?"

"Please, after you!"

Together they trudged the short distance over the plastic grass, crossing the railway track before the electric train went whistling past and onward into the little model house that had been Michelangelo's prison only a few days before.

Immediately he could see that major changes had been made to the interior. Despite the same four walls and ceiling, the dimensions of his former abode appeared ten times what he remembered. The simple furniture had been removed and replaced with a gigantic fountain that dominated the room. The impressive marble structure towered above them but the liquid that flowed over the rim of its suspended basin, cascading into the deep pool on the floor, was not water but molten white chocolate. Behind and above the fountain an oversized ornate clock in the familiar form of a Swiss cottage rested with its large doors firmly shut, presumably awaiting the top of the hour to be chimed on its clock face below.

Michelangelo spoke. "In Italy, for 30 years under the Borgias, they had warfare, terror, murder and bloodshed, but they produced me, you and the Renaissance. In Switzerland they had 500 years of democracy and peace - and what did that produce? Good clocks and bad banking. You are making me homesick of my beloved adopted land of Switzerland but tell me, what does this setting have to do with my challenge?"

"Quite simple. All you have to do is reach the timepiece and stop time."

"Stop time? You mean stop the clock? Sounds easy enough!"

"Ah, but this is no ordinary clock my old liege. This is a very special clock from Switzerland in the high summer of 1980 and you must remember that fact. Mind you, if you *can* figure out how to stop the mechanism before the chime strikes the next hour, you will have the prize of time stopping for you for a whole day. This will buy you your escape as you can easily disappear in that time with everyone frozen, just like the statues you stole. Of course though, as is part of the deal, all of your purloined goods will be returned to the Vatican by our good selves."

Michelangelo looked at the clock face. It showed the time at being six minutes to noon. "How on earth do I get up there in such a short time?"

"Simple," responded Leonardo. "At five minutes to noon a walkway will emerge from the doors above the clock face and unfurl towards you. All you have to do is climb the ramp to the top, although I grant you there may be some impediments to your progress."

Even as Leonardo finished saying those words, the minute hand reluctantly moved on to show five minutes to twelve, the shuttered doors ratcheted open and the walkway began to appear from the dark aperture like an unrolling tongue. The walkway extended towards the two men, over the top of the chocolate waterfalls, drooping slightly under its own unsupported weight as it finally met the carpet at their feet.

186

Michelangelo stepped aboard with trepidation, causing the long unsupported bridge to dip further in its middle section. Ahead he could see the wooden proboscis was now low enough to skim the top of the chocolate waterfall half way between himself and the great clock. Some of the viscous white substance flowed towards him, adhering to the wood as it cooled and hardened. Unable to resist the temptation, he walked forward to try the half-molten chocolate. The taste was divine, sweet and creamy and with a texture that melted to practically nothing on the tongue. Michelangelo gorged himself, barely noticing that the chocolate-covered platform was withdrawing itself back into the mouth beneath the clock with himself on board.

Just as the mouth was about to swallow him up, the feasting immortal jumped down onto the narrow plate that supported the large clock. There he met the life-sized figure of a woodcutter, his axe poised high above his head, motionless but clearly prepared to bring that mighty blade crashing down on the woodpile in front of him. Michelangelo, with his artistic eye, had to admit the detail on the figure was extraordinary. The character was very life-like even at close quarters and his traditional attire of braces, lederhosen that clamped his short baggy trousers against the shins and a green felt hat with a feather could all have been made by a fine tailor.

Michelangelo was gently roused from his blinkered study of the model's vestments by the gentle ticking of the clock beside him. It had now crept on to indicate it was just four minutes to noon, the gentle movement a timely reminder of his role here and now – to stop time itself. Simple enough he thought – he would just have to gain entry to the mechanism, pull out a cog or two and the hands on the clock face would cease well before noon struck.

The obvious entry point to the inside of the clock was through the shutters above the clock face, just under the sloping roof of the mock Swiss cottage. Looking up he could see a narrow "Romeo and Juliet" style balcony underneath the shutters. He wasted no time in climbing up to the balcony by easily scaling a plastic fir tree that was placed by the corner of the house. Using the rigid branches as convenient steps, he reached the top of the tree before launching himself across the small void, just as the clock moved onto three minutes to noon.

Michelangelo puffed as he tried to wedge his fingers between the shutters to pull them open. They would not budge and he started to panic when he saw the minute hand on the clock face move again. There was now only two minutes left to complete his challenge. Frantically he looked around for anything that would help him to prize open the heavy wooden doors. He looked down at the model of the woodcutter and remembered the sharp axe that he held aloft. He rushed back down the branches of the tree, nearly falling off the edge of the clock as he hurried.

With some degree of difficulty, he prized the axe from the hand of the woodcutter and rushed back up to the shutters but before he could swing back the hatchet to make the first cut, the minute hand moved to just one minute to noon and the shutters slowly began to open automatically. Laughing with relief, Michelangelo prepared to dive inside the clock as soon as the gap was wide enough to squeeze through. However, before he could dash into the dark interior, a flat circular disk slowly rotated out to meet him, a carousel complete with horses in mid-gallop. Michelangelo had no choice but to mount one of the plastic beasts and ride it as it arced back towards where it had just emerged from inside of the clock.

Despite the darkness, the whirling cogs of the clock workings were easy to see, seemingly emitting their own mysterious luminescence. Knowing there was only seconds before it was due to chime for midday he reached out and grabbed one of the smaller, slowly turning wheels, pulling it clean off its spindle and with the tension released other cogs flung from their housings as the potential energy they held was freed.

Still riding the horse as it slowed to a halt, Michelangelo held the cog high above his head like a sportsman hoisting a gilded plate in triumph. Jubilant, he jumped down from the horse, only now aware that the shutters had closed behind him. In the gloom he could make out the lines of light that showed the edges of the wooden covers and he strained at the façade once more. This time he was attempting to break out and not break in but the effort was making him dizzy and nauseous and he decided to rest a while before trying over. He wiped his brow and suddenly felt very fatigued and his last thoughts before falling into a deep sleep was that it had been a mistake eating that damn chocolate as it was almost certainly drugged. Or was it his greed and his ego that had really cost him he questioned himself. After all, he had had no need to take on these pointless challenges

Leonardo walked away and back into the real world, carefully carrying the now magically shrunken clock in one hand. He shook his head, almost disappointed that Michelangelo had not realized the trick he had played. He should have refused the challenge from the start as he had clearly told him that this was an image of Switzerland in the summer of 1980. That was the last year before Switzerland joined the rest of Europe in changing their clocks to daylight savings time and alas for Michelangelo when the clock approached noon on its great face it was already one o'clock here in Italy. Time would therefore not stop still for Michelangelo, *his* time had already run out.

EPILOGUE

After Leonardo had emerged alone from the mysterious room, Laura and Dino looked around for Michelangelo but celebrated when he did not reappear. Only Alice was a little more muted at the disappearance of her new boss and suddenly fearful of what Leonardo might do without the protection of her employer but he allayed Alice's fears saying there would be no recriminations for her treachery. Somehow she felt she could trust him, or perhaps she had little choice as she retuned her attention to her ever burgeoning bump as she felt the first twinges of contractions deep within her. Without question they all agreed to follow the enigmatic Leonardo da Vinci as he urged them to join him on a journey back to the Vatican in his flying contraption, the ornate clock secured at his side. Over the countryside they soared, back to the metropolis of Rome and the Vatican at its centre, still easily visible by the cleared grey ring of the no man's land around the tiny landlocked nation. Beyond the cleared circular band, the massed Italian troops had now been joined by impotent international peacekeeping forces.

Inside the encircled Vatican state, the new Pope, still effectively besieged by outside forces was ready. Ready to address the world once more with a simple but shocking message.

Warned only moments before, television stations once more interrupted their regular programming to bring their lucky viewers the imminent second address from the incumbent pontiff, live as it happened. Cameras trained themselves on the famous balcony, honing in on the tiny gap in the pair of curtains that concealed the entrance to the holy inner sanctum of the Pope's private quarters. The world held its breath again as the curtains twitched. The leader of the Catholic Church strode confidently towards the balcony edge. The world was now far more hesitant, confused and a little fearful after the first address and eagerly awaited an explanation or retraction for the alternative was almost unimaginable. But the Pope chose not to speak on this occasion, instead proving the old adage that actions were often far stronger than words.

And lo, millions around the world watched with utter shock as the pope put a hand to his face and appeared to slowly claw away at his skin with his nails like a crazed madman. Across the globe thousands fainted as those who could bear to keep looking saw a new face gradually revealed from beneath the old one that was now almost completely torn away and lay in shreds at the feet of the pontiff. The Papal hands then moved to the top of his head and tugged ferociously at the thin mat of grey follicles until his entire scalp lifted free to reveal a new head of long, blonde hair. The pope shook the hair free and the long luxurious locks fell down to waist level.

The pope, now almost unmistakably a woman, removed any lingering doubt as she bent down to grab the bottom of her ceremonial tunic before lifting it up on over her head and shedding it completely to show the simple blood red dress and high heels that she wore beneath.

At the exact same moment, in a concealed room in the papal quarters, Alice painlessly gave birth to a baby boy with Laura and Luca by her side. The birth of a child in the heart of the Vatican church was another abomination as far as the Holy See would be concerned and another nail in the coffin of their two-thousand year stranglehold over the Christian world. However, a few aged people who lurked in the shadows nearby knew the full implications of such a timely new arrival.

In the days and weeks that followed, story of the female pope was the only item of news across all media outlets across the world. At the same time, using the story of the millennium as a perfect cover, mysterious deliveries from Italy were made to some of the most powerful men and women across the globe. The recipients accepted their purchases with unbridled glee, even though in many cases the acquisition cost them a large chunk of their amassed fortunes and none would ever be able to show off their new prized assets outside of their heavily protected strong-rooms and even then only to their most trustworthy of guests.

One particular buyer had ordered more than most, his wealth enabling him the choicest picks of an array of almost incalculably valuable items. However, it was one item in particular he had craved, his spine tingling as he finally held the fabled but rarely understood artefact he now held in his hands.

Leonardo rued his inability to stop the redistribution of wealth from the Vatican museum and state. He had used his magical trebuchets to try to down the planes that were scattering the Vatican treasures between the world's billionaires but Michelangelo proved to be right in one regard, he did not have the power to exert such force and control from so many hundreds or even thousands of miles distant. His chagrin was not because of the loss to the church, he could not care less for their loss of power and wealth but he feared who exactly might now be wielding certain misunderstood and very powerful artefacts from the holy collection. Still, he knew that these people, if they were greedy enough, would present themselves in good time. Like pieces on a chessboard these new powerful players would take their time to work out their next move with their newly purloined toys and the it would afford them. For now though his immediate attention was drawn back to the sadly empty rooms and corridors of the Vatican, the vast spaces now appearing even larger as vacuous and blank empty cells.

He knew he would also have to address the issue of the new pope. He had to admit it was a surprise that Michelangelo had managed to conceal the fact the new head of the Roman Catholic Church, who had been fairly elected as anyone could make out from the secretive world of the selection process, was actually a woman! He wondered if the new Pope realized that her master was now again a fraction of the size he was and safely concealed in an ornate Swiss clock.

A fortnight passed before something stirred in the wreckage created from the battle wrought in a forgotten corner of St. Peter's square. Impossibly an unmarked body of a man rose from the un-cleared ashes of tanks and fire. It was the once dead figure of Luca, alive again to take his place in immortality alongside the likes of Michelangelo, Leonardo da Vinci, Joan of Arc and hundreds of unknown others across the globe.

Sic transit Gloria mundi?

www.ingramcontent.com/pod-product-compliance
Lightning Source LLC
Chambersburg PA
CBHW071311200626
46813CB00015B/1486